The Missing Piece
A Paul Phillips Mystery

By
Philip DeLizio

Copyright © 2024

All Rights Reserved

Dr. Philip DeLizio, Ed. D., is a retired schoolteacher. Upon his retirement, he decided to pursue his passion for writing.

Teen/Young Adult Inspirational Books

Rekindled Faith

Emma's Dilemma

A Light on the Horizon

Darkness to Light

A Letter of Hope

Crossroads

Paul Phillips Mysteries

Twisted Reckonings

Shadows in the Jungle

The Missing Piece

The Cricketer's Conspiracy

Shadows of the Past

Retired Detective Paul Phillips had been enjoying his quiet life on the tropical island of St. Anne until five-year-old Emma Webber was kidnapped from the beach. The head of the local police force, Sergeant Marcel Dumas, admits they are out of their depth with this carefully orchestrated crime. Against his wishes for peace, Paul's sense of duty compels him to assist with the investigation when Marcel pays him a visit.

Paul interrogates the distraught parents, Thomas, and Amelia, digging for clues within their stories. Nothing adds up and several suspicious contradictions emerge. As Paul expands his search, he discovers that Webber's marriage is far from harmonious. Thomas had been having an affair with a local woman, and a significant life insurance policy gives both lovers a motive.

When new evidence points to an insider involved in the planning, Paul focuses his search on the couple's inner circle. The island's close-knit community provides many hiding places for a kidnapper trying to evade the law. As Emma's captor becomes increasingly desperate, keeping the young girl becomes a deadly game of cat and mouse.

Driven by his experience and instincts, Paul methodically works through a growing list of suspects, carefully placed clues, and red herrings designed to mislead. With time running out for Emma, it becomes a nerve-wracking race to unravel the mystery before it's too late. After a climactic confrontation, Paul finally exposes the truth in a shocking conclusion that brings swift justice but a bittersweet end to his hoped-for retirement.

Table of Content

Chapter 1: A Violent Awakening 1

Chapter 2: Shaken Foundations 11

Chapter 3: Schemer's Masquerade 21

Chapter 4: Affairs and Insurance 32

Chapter 5: Widening the Net 47

Chapter 6: Trail Goes Cold 62

Chapter 7: Doubtful Disclosures 72

Chapter 8: Targeted Search 82

Chapter 9: Confronting the Calm 89

Chapter 10: Frayed Nerves 104

Chapter 11: Closer than Known 120

Chapter 12 Aftermath 139

Chapter 13: Old Wounds, New Beginnings 151

Chapter 14: Full Circle 164

Chapter 1

A Violent Awakening

The Caribbean... it's a paradise but shadows lurked beneath the sunny facade. The beaches, pristine and inviting, were a stark contrast to the darkness that sometimes washed ashore. The sand was golden and warm beneath your feet, a reminder of the calm before the storm. And the sun, relentless in its brilliance, cast both light and shadows on this beautiful yet troubled island. It's a place where beauty conceals danger, where one must tread carefully to uncover the truth.

St. Anne, Paul Phillip's adopted home. It's a small yet vibrant island in the heart of the Caribbean, where the lush greenery meets the crystal-clear waters that hug its shores. The town exuded a quaint charm, with colorful buildings that lined the cobblestone streets, telling stories of years gone by. The locals, warm and welcoming, had woven a tapestry of traditions and legends that permeated every corner of the island. The rhythm of life here was slow and steady, like the gentle sway of the palm trees in the ocean breeze.

Philip DeLizio

The pulsing beat of the music at the local taverns blended with the laughter of children that played in the streets created a symphony of island life. St. Anne was a place where time seems to have stood still, yet beneath its tranquil surface lay a tapestry of secrets waiting to be unraveled. Living here, amid the beauty and mystery, reminded Paul that even in paradise, darkness could take root if left unchecked.

The French influence on St. Anne was unmistakable. From the charming architecture that reflected a blend of French and Caribbean styles to the mouthwatering cuisine that married flavors from both worlds, the island bore the marks of its colonial past. The locals, proud of their heritage, speak a melodic mix of French and Creole, which adds a musical cadence to everyday conversations.

The French culture had seeped into the very fabric of life on the island, shaping traditions, festivals, and customs that were celebrated with passion and gusto. Whether it was the lively street markets that brimmed with fresh produce or the colorful carnival parades that lit up the town square, the French influence was evident in every aspect of daily life. Living here, among this vibrant tapestry of cultures, reminded Paul of the rich history that weaved through every corner of this enchanting island.

The tropical sun rose warm on Paul's face as he awoke to the familiar sounds of island life drifting through the sea breeze. Stretching with satisfaction, he savored another lazy morning in this palm-fringed paradise that had become his quiet home. The best part about living on a Caribbean beach, according to Paul, is the sense of freedom it brings.

The endless expanse of the ocean stretching out before you, the soothing sound of the waves lulling you into a peaceful state of mind. The sea breeze carried whispers of adventure and mystery, which mingled with the salty scent of the ocean.

The sunrise in the Caribbean was a sight to behold. As the first light crept over the horizon, it painted the sky in hues of pink, orange, and gold. The gentle waves reflected the colors like a mirror, creating a mesmerizing dance of light and shadow on the water. It was a moment of calm before the day's chaos began a brief respite in a world full of mysteries waiting to be unraveled. And the spectacular sunsets that paint the sky in a riot of colors, a reminder that even in darkness, beauty can be found. Living here, in nature's raw beauty, reminded Paul that even in the most tranquil places, chaos can still find a way in.

After getting dressed in shorts and a t-shirt, he started breakfast of eggs, fruit, and strong coffee. Local songs played softly on the radio as always, soothing island melodies. News reports brought no trouble, just weather, and festivals. "All remains well in our tranquil community," the radio assured listeners. A rueful smile ghosted Paul's lip. If only it were true.

He tried focusing on routines, not letting any foreboding cloud the sky. But as Paul ate, memories intruded, and past crimes obliterated innocence with brutal efficiency. Another victim needed his skills to find justice, which endangered the calm that blanketed this sheltered place. Its people lived simple, untroubled lives while he coursed dark streets hunting predators. Could he shield them still?

As he fetched his coffee, the movement on the beach below caught his eye. People were running toward the water's edge, gesturing wildly. His detective's intuition ignited a spark of concern, this was no ordinary activity. Shielding his gaze from the sun, he scanned the surf and saw a frantic man wading back and forth, splashing violently as others shouted. He sat down his cup and hurried out the front door wearing just his shorts, t-shirt, and no shoes, and out onto the sand.

"What's happened?", he asked the gathered onlookers, who were now joined by more alarmed faces. A distraught woman collapsed sobbing into another's arms. A man turned to Paul, panting. "It's Emma Webber...she's missing! One moment she was building castles, the next just...gone!"

Dread pooled in Paul's stomach. This was no accident. Someone had taken that little girl from her kingdom of sand. He tried to soothe the crowd as the local police arrived, knowing their panic could contaminate clues. Through the chaos Sergeant Dumas appeared, solemnly meeting Paul's eyes. "We need your help, my friend. This is no ordinary missing person's case."

Paul nodded, steeling himself once more for the hunt. His tropical paradise had been shattered, and a new case had unfolded, one that would test both his skills, and his retirement's fragile peace. Paul breathed deeply. There, daily sun saluted and posed, keeping his aging body lithe amid island leisure.

In the city where Paul was from, dawn brought another damaged body demanding justice. But here in paradise were only the songs of birds, the laughter of children and adults, and surf, nature's cure that healed wounds the world had inflicted. For six peaceful months, Paul had immersed himself in this rhythmic life, leaving violence and its aftermath behind locked files. Six peaceful months since his last case helping the local police department. It too was a missing person's case. A mystery of a fellow islander gone missing.

As he delved into that case, Paul uncovered secrets that powerful people were willing to kill to keep hidden. With his determination to seek the truth, Paul found himself in the crosshairs of dangerous enemies who wanted the case closed permanently. Now its shadow fell across his beach, and duty called him back into the fray, hoping this case would be easier to solve. And less dangerous.

Paul readied himself once more. His gift was needed. This girl's plea could not be denied. He would maintain safety here as diligently as serving any city. With a last glance at the waves and sky, Paul hurried to meet the sergeant and learn what shadows now plagued their paradise.

The sun hung low in the sky as it cast a warm glow over the crystal-clear waters that lapped gently at the sandy shore. Seagulls circled overhead, their cries mingled with the distant chatter of tourists oblivious to the tragedy that had struck.

The salt-tinged breeze carried a sense of unease, a stark reminder that even paradise could harbor dark secrets. Amid the picturesque backdrop, the presence of frantic onlookers and concerned locals added a somber note to the usual tranquility of the beach. It was as if the peaceful façade of the island had been shattered, revealing the harsh reality that even in paradise, danger lurked.

His tranquil days were truly shattered now. A predator stalked their island, and he would find him before he claimed another victim. This time, he would not fail.

Sergeant Dumas arrived, urgency shadowed his normally genial features. The beach now sectioned off as Paul listened grimly to the Webbers' shaken accounts. "One-minute building castles as always, laughing...then gone!"

Amelia Webber wept into her husband's chest. Paul watched discreetly, his intuition tingled. Something troubled Paul as he watched and listened to the Webber's tone. Something was amiss with their display of emotions. Thomas paced, chain-smoking. "We only looked away for a moment...how did anyone take her so fast?"

Dumas' brow furrowed deeper. "This was no opportunist, the planning involved is unprecedented here."

Paul joined the sergeant hoping his experience offered answers this good man lacked. But the crime tore all logic, no trace of any evidence, save a child's toy and a family shredded by unknown motives.

Dumas sighed heavily. "Whoever this fiend is, they certainly covered their tracks well. I am afraid we are lost without your skills, my friend. Are you willing to assist us in finding who did this, and why?"

Paul nodded solemnly. Nightmares ruled here now, and he would chase each shadow till dawn. Paul watched neighbors comfort the grief-stricken couple as his instincts were telling him the Webbers were telling the whole story. Street-smarts told him these good people, unused to malice, floundered in the darkness that was now descending.

As the crowd dispersed reluctantly, Dumas drew Paul aside. His eyes reflected the community's trust and betrayed his private doubts. "This crime goes deeper than any we've seen, mon ami. We are out of our depth."

Paul understood the admission took guts and failure. Terrified leaders tasked with protecting others. Yet security came from facing truth, not false bravado. He placed a steadying hand on Dumas' shoulder. "I promise to give it my all, sergeant. If I can help it, this crime will not go unsolved. I'll use all my resources and skills to assist in the best way I know how, and together, we will spare the town any further pain. We'll find the bastard who did this."

Dumas sighed gratefully. "Your willingness and experience give us hope, my friend. Please, help us make sense of this madness before anyone else suffers. I don't know if this is any isolated case or the beginning of something else. I'll leave the case in your capable hands."

This tranquil island had become Paul's comfort, its peace mended scars from a life of tracking monsters. Yet those demons found even these peaceful shores now, and one little angel had suffered their vengeful wrath. How he yearned to sink back into those sun-kissed days!

As Paul stood on the beach, the warm sun on his skin, the sound of the waves crashed against the shore, but his mind was elsewhere. The image of little Emma Webber's distraught parents, the desperation in their eyes, brought back a flood of memories he thought he'd left behind. Unsolved crimes, cases that still haunted him, and the weight of justice unfulfilled.

His mind wandered back to the case of the Riverview Murders, a case from his past as a police detective in the U. S. Three young women, all in their early twenties, found dead in their homes, each with a small, silver cross placed on their chest. The police department was stumped, and he was the lead detective on the case. He poured his heart and soul into it but was never able to catch the killer. The last victim, Sarah, was the one that still kept him up at night. He remembered her mother, broken and devastated, as she pleaded with Paul to find her daughter's killer.

He failed her. He failed all of them.

The Missing Piece: A Paul Phillips Mystery

The Larkin Abduction was another case that still lingered in his mind. A seven-year-old boy was taken from his front yard, and never found. The investigation was a marathon, but the police never got a lead and never found a shred of evidence that could point them to the kidnapper. The Larkin family was destroyed, and Paul was left with the guilt of not being able to bring their son home.

And then, there was the Silk Street Arsons. A series of fires ravaged the city's commercial district, leaving a trail of destruction and loss. Paul suspected an organized crime syndicate, but he could never pin them down. The fires stopped as suddenly as they started, but the memories of the devastation, the charred remains of people's livelihoods, still lingered.

These cases, and many more like them, were the driving force behind his need to solve new crimes. They were constant reminders that justice is not always served and that there were still voices that needed to be heard. The weight of those unsolved crimes was crushing at times, but it's also what fueled his determination to uncover the truth.

Paul knew that he was not the same detective he used to be. The years had taken their toll, and the scars of his past failures were still fresh. But he also knew that he had a unique perspective, a perspective that could help him see the unseen, to connect the dots that others might miss. And he was willing to use that perspective to bring justice to those who needed it, no matter the cost.

The case of Emma Webber's kidnapping was a reminder that Paul was not done yet. He may have retired from the force, but he was not retired from seeking justice. The memories of his past failures would continue to haunt him, but they would also drive him to push forward, fight for the truth, and bring closure to those who needed it.

The past could not, would not, be forgotten.

As he stood on the beach, he knew that he had to do everything in his power to find Emma Webber. He owed it to her, to her parents, and to the ghosts of his past. The memories of those unsolved crimes would continue to haunt him, but they would also fuel his determination to solve this case, to bring justice to those who need it, and to find redemption for his own failures.

This case struck a sour note for Paul. The memories that plagued his restless nights were like ghosts from his darkened past. These memories clung to Paul's soul like shadows that refused to fade, driving him to seek redemption in a world stained with darkness.

Chapter 2
Shaken Foundations

Later that day, Paul pulled up outside the Webber family home, a grand waterfront mansion perched on a hill overlooking the turquoise waters of the sea. The Webber mansion stood proudly amid the lush tropical foliage, a grand yet imposing structure that spoke of wealth and privilege. The mansion itself was an architectural marvel, with sweeping verandas adorned with intricately carved railings and vibrant tropical flowers that spilled from elegant planters. The whitewashed walls gleamed in the sunlight, a stark contrast to the vibrant greenery that surrounded it.

As Paul stepped onto the manicured grounds, he was met with the sweet fragrance of exotic blooms that mingled with the salty tang of the nearby ocean. The sprawling gardens unfolded before him, a tapestry of colors and textures that seemed to stretch endlessly toward the horizon. Palms swayed gently in the breeze, their fronds whispering secrets borne on the wind.

From the vantage point of the mansion's terrace, the view was nothing short of breathtaking. Beyond the emerald lawns and meandering pathways, the azure waters of the Caribbean stretched out to meet the distant horizon, merging seamlessly with the clear blue sky above. It was a scene of tranquility and beauty, a stark contrast to the turmoil that simmered beneath the surface of the Webber family's facade.

As he walked up the stone pathway lined with tropical flowers, Paul hardened himself for what was sure to be an emotional encounter. Through the ornate French doors, he could see Amelia sobbing uncontrollably on the sofa as Thomas paced back and forth, running his hands through his hair. The elegant parlor looked like a scene of chaos, with photo frames shattered on the marble floors and furniture overturned. Paul knocked gently and Thomas flung open the door, his bloodshot eyes showing a mixture of anguish and anger. "Have you found who did this?" he demanded. Paul shook his head somberly and introduced himself, saying he was there to ask some routine questions.

Thomas Webber cut a striking figure, with his tall, lean frame that exuded an air of sophistication and wealth. His impeccably tailored suits clung to his athletic build, emphasizing his stature in the community as a successful businessman. Despite his outward charm, there was a steely resolve in his piercing gaze that hinted at a man accustomed to getting what he wanted.

As the head of a prominent corporation on the island, Thomas

Webber commanded respect and influence that extended far beyond the confines of his lavish mansion. His job as a wealthy businessman afforded him a veneer of respectability, hiding the darker truths that lurked beneath the polished facade. Behind closed doors, Thomas's true nature emerged, revealing a man entangled in a web of deceit and betrayal that threatened to unravel the very fabric of his carefully constructed life.

His demeanor was a curious blend of charm and aloofness, a calculated mask that he wore to shield his secrets from prying eyes. His suave exterior belied a turbulent inner world beset by guilt and regret, a man haunted by the choices he had made and the consequences that followed. Despite his composed facade, there was a hint of vulnerability in his eyes, a crack in the armor that hinted at a soul tormented by inner demons.

Webber was in his late forties, with a distinguished air that spoke of experience and wisdom beyond his years. His graying temples and lines etched around his eyes hinted at a life lived fully, marked by both triumphs and tribulations. Thomas Webber was a man of contradictions, a complex tapestry of ambition and despair that unraveled slowly in the face of scrutiny and truth.

Paul was led into the parlor, where Amelia was being comforted by a neighbor. She looked up with tear-stained cheeks as Paul entered and let out an involuntary whimper. "Please, tell us anything you know that could help," Thomas pleaded, his voice betraying an edge of impatience.

Paul sat across from the grieving parents and said gently, "I understand this is incredibly difficult. But answering a few questions could provide invaluable clues. I promise we will catch whoever has done this terrible thing." He pulled out his notepad, hoping their raw emotions might reveal buried truths. Thomas recounted finding Emma missing from the beach around noon and raised an immediate alarm before frantically searching with neighbors and calling the police. But Amelia said she last saw Emma playing in the yard at 10 am before doing some gardening.

"That can't be right, I told you I took her to the beach myself," Thomas insisted impatiently.

Amelia shook her head, fresh tears spilling down her cheeks. "No, she was in the backyard this morning, I'm sure of it."

Paul sensed the pending argument and interjected, "Memories can be unclear during traumatic times. The small details aren't as vital now as finding who took Emma. Is there anyone who might wish your family harm?"

Thomas shrugged dismissively. But Amelia glanced nervously at her husband before replying, "We keep to ourselves mostly. But money can breed envy in a small place..." Her implied meaning was unmistakable. While the couple seemed understandably distraught, Paul knew emotion could veil darker truths.

Thomas began pacing feverishly again as Amelia broke into a fresh bout of tears. "I just don't understand how someone could do this," he muttered, more to himself than Paul.

Amelia possessed a serene beauty, her delicate features framed by cascading waves of chestnut hair touched with hints of silver. Her soft, hazel eyes held a depth of emotion, reflecting both strength and vulnerability in equal measure. Despite the turmoil that surrounded her, there was a quiet grace to her presence, a sense of resilience that belied the pain she carried within.

In contrast to her husband's commanding presence, Amelia's job as a dedicated mother defined her in ways that transcended conventional roles. Her unwavering commitment to her child shone through in every interaction, normally a pillar of strength upon which her family relied. The subtle lines etched on her face hinted at the sacrifices she had made, the silent battles fought in the name of love and protection.

Her demeanor was usually a study in poise and composure, a mask worn to shield her innermost thoughts from prying eyes. She exuded a quiet dignity that masked a well of untold emotions, a woman grappling with the weight of secrets too heavy to bear alone. Despite the challenges that beset her, there was a steely resolve in her gaze, a resolve to protect her loved ones at any cost. Amelia was in her early forties, with a timeless elegance that transcended mere numbers. Her graceful movements and understated charm hinted at a life lived with purpose and integrity, a woman defined not by her age but by the depth of her character. Amelia Webber was a study in contrasts, a portrait of strength and vulnerability painted on the canvas of her soul.

Seeing an opportunity while Thomas was distracted, Paul leaned closer to Amelia. "I want to help find who took Emma," he said gently. "Is there anything else I should know?" Amelia glanced fearfully at her husband's back before meeting Paul's gaze. Her hands trembled in her lap as she gave the faintest nod. But before she could speak, Thomas spun around abruptly.

"My wife needs rest. This interrogation can wait," he snapped, though Paul had asked no new questions. He took Amelia's arm in what seemed a painful grip. "Come, dear."

As they left the room, Paul noticed Amelia's pleading look over her shoulder. He now sensed tension underneath the couple's obvious anguish, though their reasons remained cloaked. Only further investigation would reveal the troubling truths behind this tragedy. While Thomas grew impatient and evasive, redirecting lines of inquiry, Amelia responded nervously but offered one potentially revealing nugget when alone. Paul sensed her fearfulness stemmed more from her husband's reactions than grief.

Their account of Emma's disappearance differed in key details, from the timeline to her last known whereabouts. Whereas Amelia trembled under Thomas's watch, he maintained an angry defensiveness throughout. The undercurrent of tension between them was unmistakable. Most troubling was the furtive pleading in Amelia's eyes as she was whisked from the room. Paul wondered what secret truths were silenced by duty or danger, imprisoning her under Thomas's control. This kidnapping had shattered more than one family; motives and deceptions lay just beneath the surface of their polished public images.

As Paul navigated the winding road that hugged the coastline of St. Anne, the warm tropical sun beating down on his car, he couldn't shake off the feeling that he'd just missed something crucial in that interview. The Webber's house seemed like a facade, a carefully constructed mask that hid a multitude of secrets.

His mind replayed the conversation with Amelia and Thomas, trying to dissect every word, every gesture. Amelia's hesitance, the way she glanced at Thomas before speaking, told Paul that she was hiding something. But what was it? And why did Thomas seem so adamant about controlling the narrative? He made a mental note to keep a close eye on him, to see if he could uncover what was driving Webber's behavior.

The road twisted and turned, the sea breeze carried the sweet scent of blooming flowers and the distant sound of surf crashing against the shore. Paul rolled down the window to let the warm air fill his car as he gazed out at the turquoise water. The island's beauty was a stark contrast to the darkness that lurked beneath its surface.

As he approached the intersection that led to his small beachside bungalow, he couldn't help but think about the case that had brought him out of retirement, again. Emma's disappearance was a grim reminder that evil didn't take a vacation, not even in a tropical paradise. Paul's gut told him that this was more than just a simple kidnapping, that there were layers to this case that he had yet to uncover.

He pulled into his driveway, the sound of the gravel crunching beneath his tires, a familiar comfort. As he stepped out of the car, the warm sun on my skin, he made a silent promise to himself: he would find Emma, no matter what secrets he had to uncover, no matter what demons he had to face.

With a deep breath, he walked towards his bungalow, the sound of the waves and the cries of seagulls faded into the background as he delved deeper into the case.

Paul sat up late into the night, poring over case files by lamplight. Sitting on his porch, he gazed out over the moonlit ocean as he replayed the day's tragic events in his mind. Reviewing his notes from questioning the Webbers, contradictions, and unease emerged more clearly. Sifting through witness statements and Sergeant Dumas' initial crime scene report, discrepancies emerged between the evidence and the Webbers' recollections.

According to neighbors, Thomas was golfing miles away when Emma was allegedly taken from the beach just past noon. No physical evidence or footprints supported a beach kidnapping either. But the trauma of loss could distort perception. Paul knew not to make assumptions based on surface inconsistencies alone. However, the reason he doubted Emma was kidnapped from the beach was due to the absence of any solid witnesses or evidence pointing to a struggle at the beach. No one heard screams or saw any suspicious activity that would indicate a kidnapping took place right there.

It struck Paul as odd that such a brazen act could occur in broad daylight without a trace left behind. His gut told him there was more to this puzzle than a simple snatch from the beach. A deeper and more nuanced investigation was critical to understand all perspectives in such an emotionally charged case.

He would need to carefully compare each new detail to build a full picture, however uncomfortable truths might challenge initial impressions. Only then would the real sequence of events come into focus, concealed motives emerge, and little Emma receive the justice she deserved. This complex mystery demanded approaching each thread methodically and with an open mind. Paul resolved to untangle the varied strands that lead to the heart of the case with patience and precision.

He ate his dinner alone on the porch, gazing out at the moonlit sea as its gentle rhythm soothed his restless mind. Yet troubling questions remained. What motive drove such a heinous crime in their picturesque community? Ransom seemed likely, given the family's wealth. However, a sinister alternative emerged if evidence contradicted the beach abduction.

And who among their close-knit neighbors could be twisted enough to harm an innocent child? To bring justice for Emma demanded confronting disturbing secrets and motives. Paul sensed unraveling this case would crack open wounds buried deep within familiar bonds.

He fortified his resolve, knowing the path ahead would test his skills, and that paradise often concealed nightmares. Only by facing the island's shadows could he banish this threat and restore the safety shattered by one evil act. At this point, Paul had interviewed the Webber family and uncovered inconsistencies in their statements, as well as tensions within their relationship. By carefully analyzing clues and considering different possibilities, he sought to untangle this complex case and do right by little Emma.

Chapter 3
Schemer's Masquerade

At first light, Paul slipped silently through the dense foliage bordering the Webber estate. He settled into a concealed crouching position behind a large banyan tree and retrieved his binoculars from their padded case. Sweeping the landscape methodically, he soon spotted movement near the manor house.

Thomas paced the veranda restlessly, smoking cigarette after cigarette as he glanced repeatedly at his watch. When Amelia emerged wraith-like onto the porch, clutching her robe tightly against the chill, Thomas barked something harshly. She flinched at his sharp tone, tears welling fresh in her reddened eyes. As Amelia began to speak, Thomas cut her off with a curt gesture and strode past without meeting her anguished gaze.

Paul observed their rigid exchange closely, capturing telling details through his lenses. Thomas's agitated energy hinted at his fraying nerves, while Amelia seemed to shrink more by the moment. Their tangled tension served only to heighten Paul's suspicions regarding the truth lying beneath the Webber's polished veneer. He would maintain a discreet watch for clues to their private storms, unlocking the mysteries shrouding innocent Emma's brutal fate.

Paul shadowed Thomas as he strode purposefully to his Mercedes. Following discreetly in his own vehicle, Paul tracked the gleaming sedan along Serpentine Road as it snaked deeper into the forested hills. Thomas drove with a stony focus, oblivious to the twisting curves ahead.

As thick foliage closed densely around the winding route, Paul dropped further back to remain unobserved. Through sweeping bends clinging to sheer cliff sides, he eyed Thomas's tense profile intently. The man's furrowed brow and tight jaw spoke of roiling thoughts better left unexplored, fueling Paul's suspicions. Where was Thomas going in such a hurry? And why is he going alone?

Rounding a hairpin turn at reckless speed, Thomas's car vanished abruptly from sight. Paul accelerated in pursuit, only to brake hard upon finding the Mercedes parked on a remote overlook. He watched unseen as Thomas stalked to the cliff's edge, lighting another cigarette with hands that trembled. Paul was determined to uncover the truth as he maintained a stealthy watch from the shaded tree line as Thomas marched toward the shore below.

A striking brunette beauty emerged from the corner of the beach, hidden from the road, sparking a passionate embrace upon seeing

Thomas Webber. Her long, flowing hair seemed to dance in the tropical breeze, and her eyes held a depth that belied her outward grace. She was clad in a flowing white sundress that billowed around her like the frothy sea foam. The fabric clung to her graceful form, accentuating her every movement as she walked along the shoreline, her bare feet leaving delicate imprints in the sand. Her long, dark hair cascaded down her back in lustrous waves, highlighted by the sunlight dancing upon the water droplets that clung to its strands.

Despite the weight of the situation, her appearance was a serene contrast to the turmoil of the investigation. A siren among the palm trees drew Thomas into turbulent waters he couldn't resist. But beauty often conceals the darkest secrets, as Paul has come to learn. Their kiss deepened with raw hunger, Thomas grasping the unnamed woman as if drowning.

He discreetly snapped photos capturing the incriminating intimacy without being seen. Paul processed the damning evidence with icy calculation.

Thomas's poorly concealed affair blew a hole in his grief-stricken portrayal, rousing grave suspicions regarding his faithless marriage. The insurance policy amplified motivation for murder, Paul now marked the errant spouse as a prime suspect awaiting interrogation.

Retrieving his stored equipment, Paul returned to his car and headed back toward town to review the photo proof of duplicity in Thomas Webber's charade of sorrow.

Paul thought it was time to revisit Amelia while Thomas wasn't home.

He stood at the Webber's doorstep, the photographs still fresh in his mind, the evidence of Thomas's infidelity burning a hole in his pocket. He took a deep breath, steeling himself for the conversation that was to come.

Amelia answered the door, her eyes red-rimmed, her skin pale. She looked like she hadn't slept in days.

"Amelia, may I have a word with you?" Paul asked, his tone gentle but firm.

She nodded, stepping aside to let Paul in. They walked into the living room, the same room where he had interviewed them both just days before. The atmosphere was heavier now, weighted by the secrets he had uncovered.

"Amelia, I need to show you something," he said, pulling out his camera with the photos he had taken. "I took these photos a short time ago. Do you recognize the people in the picture?"

Her eyes widened as she took in the images, her gaze fixed on Thomas and his mistress. The color drained from her face, leaving her skin a ghostly pale.

"Where...where did you get these?" she stammered, her voice barely above a whisper.

"I followed Thomas as he left here a few minutes ago, Amelia. I know about Thomas's affair," he said with a sympathetic voice.

She looked up at me, her eyes brimming with tears. "I didn't know," she whispered, her voice cracking. "I didn't know it was still going on."

Paul handed her a tissue, and she took it, her hands shook as she dabbed at her eyes.

"Can you tell me anything about Thomas's affair?" he asked, his notebook and pen at the ready. "How long has it been going on?"

Amelia took a deep breath, her eyes flashing with anger. "It started about six months ago. I thought it was over, but I guess I was wrong."

"And did you know about the life insurance policy?" he pressed on, his eyes locked on hers.

Her gaze dropped, her voice barely above a whisper. "Yes, I knew about it. Thomas said it was for our protection, but...but I didn't know it was so much."

Paul nodded, his mind racing with the implications. This changed everything. The motives, the suspects, the entire case.

"Amelia, I need to ask you something," he said, his tone gentle but firm. "Do you think Thomas is capable of hurting Emma?"

Her eyes snapped up, her face pale. "No, no, he would never hurt her," she said, her voice laced with conviction. "He loves her, Paul. He loves her more than anything."

Paul nodded, his mind still racing with the possibilities. But as he looked at Amelia, he saw something there, something she wasn't saying. And he knew he had to keep pushing, to uncover the truth that lay hidden beneath the surface.

Still sitting in the living room, deep in conversation with Amelia, the door burst open and Thomas stormed in. His face was red with anger, his eyes blazing with fury.

"What are you doing here?" he yelled, his voice echoing off the walls. "You have no right to be here!"

Before Paul could react, Webber grabbed Paul by the arm, his grip like a vice. Paul felt a surge of adrenaline as he tried to shake him off, but he held tight.

"I'm making it my business, Thomas," he said, his voice cool and calm, despite the heat of the situation. "I'm investigating your daughter's disappearance, and I won't be intimidated by you."

Thomas's face twisted in rage, his eyes bulging with fury. "You're just trying to pin this on me, aren't you? You're just trying to ruin my life!"

Amelia stood up, her voice trembling. "Thomas, stop. Let him go."

But Thomas didn't relent. He kept yelling, his voice growing louder and more menacing. "You're just a retired detective, Phillips. You're just a washed-up has-been trying to make a name for yourself."

Paul felt a spark of anger ignite within him, but he kept his cool. He knew that Thomas was trying to provoke him, to get Paul to react. But he wasn't going to give him the satisfaction.

"I'm not going to play games with you, Thomas," he said, his voice firm but controlled. "I'm going to find out what happened to Emma, and if you're involved, I'll make sure you pay for it."

Thomas's grip on Paul's arm tightened, his fingernails digging deep into his skin. But still, Paul didn't flinch. he just stared Webber down, his eyes locked on his.

Amelia intervened again, her voice firm. "Thomas, let him go. This isn't helping."

Thomas's grip slowly loosened, and Paul pulled his arm free. "I'm not going to let you bully me, Thomas," he said. "I'm going to find out the truth, no matter what you do."

Thomas's face was still red with anger, but Paul could see the fear lurking beneath the surface. He knew Paul was getting close to something, and he was scared.

Paul turned to Amelia, his voice soft. "I'll be in touch, Amelia. We'll talk more about this later."

And with that, he walked out of the house, leaving Thomas's anger and Amelia's tears behind.

That evening, after receiving a phone call from Amelia, Paul returned to the Webber house.

As he arrived at the Webber house, the sun had dipped below the horizon, casting a warm orange glow over the island. Amelia answered the door, her eyes red-rimmed, her face pale. It was apparent she had been crying.

"Amelia, what's going on?" Paul asked, his tone gentle. "You wanted to talk to me about Thomas's affair?"

She nodded, her voice barely above a whisper. "Yes, Paul. I need to tell you everything. It's been eating away at me, and I can't keep it inside anymore."

He followed her into the living room, the same room where they had spoken earlier. But this time, the atmosphere was different. Amelia seemed more relaxed, more open.

"Tell me, Amelia," he said, his voice encouraging. "What's been going on in your marriage?"

Amelia took a deep breath, her eyes dropped to the floor. "It's been a long time since Thomas and I were happy, Paul. We used to be so in love, but over the years, we just...drifted apart."

"I see," he said, as he had his notebook and pen at the ready. "Can you tell me more about that?"

Amelia nodded, her voice gaining strength. "We used to have so much in common, but as Emma grew older, we started to grow apart. Thomas became more and more distant, and I didn't know how to reach him. We started to argue more, and...and then I found out about the affair."

"I'm sorry, Amelia," Paul said, his voice soft. "That must have been devastating for you."

Amelia's eyes welled up with tears, but she didn't cry. "It was, Paul. It was like my whole world had been turned upside down. I didn't know what to do, or how to make it stop."

He nodded, his mind raced with the implications. "And how did you feel about Thomas's affair?" he asked, my tone gentle.

Amelia's voice dropped into a whisper. "I felt betrayed. I felt like I wasn't enough for him, like he didn't love me anymore. And then...and then I started to wonder if he was capable of doing something to Emma."

Paul leaned forward, his eyes locked on hers. "Do you think Thomas is capable of hurting Emma?"

Amelia's gaze dropped, her voice barely above a whisper. "I don't know, Paul. I don't know what he's capable of anymore. But I do know that I'm scared, and I need your help to find out what happened to my daughter."

He nodded, his heart going out to her. "I'll do everything I can,

Amelia. I promise you that."

And with that, Paul left the Webber house, his mind raced with the new information, his heart heavy with the weight of Amelia's secrets.

As he walked back to his car, Paul couldn't help but think about the conversation he had just had with Amelia. The weight of her secrets, the pain of her betrayal, it was all so heavy, so overwhelming.

He couldn't help but think about Thomas, about how he had manipulated and deceived his wife. The affair, the lies, the pain he had caused Amelia. It was all so calculated, so deliberate. But as he drove home, his mind started to wander back to Emma. The little girl who was still missing, the victim of a crime that seemed to get more and more complex by the minute. He thought about Amelia's fears, about her doubts about Thomas's capabilities. Was he capable of hurting Emma? He didn't know, but he knew he had to find out.

As he pulled into his driveway, Paul couldn't help but feel a sense of responsibility, a sense of duty to find Emma and bring her home. He knew it wouldn't be easy, but he was determined to see it through.

As he walked into his house, his mind still raced with thoughts and questions. He knew he had to get to the bottom of this, to uncover the truth behind Emma's disappearance. He poured himself a glass of Island rum, his mind still reeled from the conversation with Amelia. He knew it would be a long road ahead, but he was ready for it.

He sat down on his couch, his eyes fixed on the wall, as his mind was filled with possibilities. He knew he had to keep pushing, to keep digging, until he found the truth. And as he sat there, lost in thought, Paul knew that he would do everything in his power to find Emma, to bring her home safe and sound.

Chapter 4

Affairs and Insurance

The morning sun shone brightly as Paul walked down the quiet street of Rue des Palms, in Belle Anse, a charming little town, toward the insurance office. Belle Anse was a picturesque gem nestled on the coast of St. Anne. The blend of French elegance and Caribbean charm truly made it a unique setting for Paul's investigation. Along the street, there were quaint cafes serving rich Caribbean coffee, a colorful boutique that sold handmade jewelry, and a local art gallery showcasing vibrant paintings. The buildings indeed reflected the French Caribbean heritage with their pastel-colored walls, intricate ironwork balconies, and lush tropical plants adorning the facades.

His mind churned with questions about the curious life insurance policy taken out on little Emma. He slipped inside the building that housed the insurance company. It was a grand colonial building with white-washed walls and a red-tiled roof that gleamed under the Caribbean sun. Tall, arched windows framed by intricate wrought-iron railings added a touch of old-world charm to the facade. A carved wooden sign above the entrance proudly displayed the company's name in elegant script, hinting at a long-standing reputation for reliability and trustworthiness.

As Paul stepped inside, the cool interior offered a respite from the tropical heat, with polished wooden floors and antique furnishings that spoke of a history steeped in tradition.

Once inside, he introduced himself to the receptionist. "I'm investigating a case and need details on any policies held by Thomas and Amelia Webber." The woman typed slowly, clicking her tongue. "Let me pull those files up for you now, Officer...?"

"Retired Detective Paul Phillips, on loan to the local police department" he replied.

The receptionist was a bit hesitant at first when Paul requested information, understandably so since Paul no longer held official authority as a retired detective. However, once he explained the gravity of the situation and the potential implications for the case, she eventually softened and cooperated, albeit with a lingering wariness in her eyes. Paul smiled, thinking it's all about how you present yourself and the urgency of the matter that can sway people, even in the face of regulations.

She printed the records and Paul pored over them intently. A sizable whole-life policy on Thomas proved unremarkable, but the new accidental death riders on Emma and Amelia raised red flags. Only a month old with Thomas as the sole beneficiary, it reeked of ulterior motives. Paul thanked the receptionist and exited the building, disturbed by this latest implication of Thomas's deceit. Motive and means existed in equal measure it seemed, yet solid proof remained elusive.

Paul vowed to untangle the twisted threads surrounding Emma's disappearance and find justice for the vibrant and young little girl. The game had only begun, and Paul intended to win. He pondered this troubling new information as he strode down the avenue.

On a hunch, as Paul was halfway down the block, he phoned the insurance office once more. After a few inquiries, the receptionist said "Just a moment, let me check...yes, it seems Mr. Webber increased the accidental death benefit on his wife's policy last week. He's still listed as the sole beneficiary in case of an 'unforeseen tragedy'."

Unease crept up Paul's spine. Two new policies, both payable to Thomas alone, should harm befall his family. It painted a damning portrait of the man's integrity. Paul recalled Amelia's fear and Thomas's evasions. Only a killer could benefit so vastly from his loved ones' demises. Resolve hardened in Paul's gut. By any means, he would expose the true rogue endangering this community. No amount of money or lies would suffice, only the raw truth could ensure justice for Emma. The game had drawn its first blood, and Paul refused to let more fall before the culprit faced retribution under the law.

Paul sped to the stately Webber estate, with stern intentions. Paul's car is not simply a means of transportation, but a reflection of his character. This gem was not his green Jeep, instead, it was a classic 1969 Ford Mustang Fastback, a sleek and powerful machine that had weathered the years with grace. The vibrant red paint gleamed under the tropical sun, hinting at the thrilling journeys it had taken Paul on. Every curve and line of this vintage beauty told a story of speed, precision, and timeless elegance. It may not be the newest model, but it held a special place in his heart for its reliability and enduring style.

Arriving back at the Webber Estate, Paul stormed up to the front doors of the manor, knocked loudly and persistently, and when the butler answered, Paul demanded he fetch his employer. The butler was taken aback at Paul's insistence and what he deemed a rude demand.

Mr. Jenkins is a man of impeccable manners, always dressed in a crisply pressed black suit that spoke to his attention to detail. His grey hair was neatly combed back, framing a face that held years of loyal service etched in its lines. Mr. Jenkins moved with quiet efficiency, anticipating the needs of the family before they even voiced them. His presence in the Webber household was like a finely tuned orchestra, ensuring that everything ran smoothly behind the scenes.

Thomas appeared, languid as a ghost. "More questions, Detective?"

"You took out life insurance policies on your family, with you as sole beneficiary," Paul stated. The accusation burned in his eyes.

Thomas stiffened, face contorting into a grimace. "I simply prepare for uncertainties."

"You used your daughter's kidnapping for your financial gain!" Paul roared. "Where is she, Thomas? What have you done with Emma?"

At this, Thomas blanched ghastly white. Without uttering a defense, he spun on his heel and fled.

Paul stood in the Webber's living room, his eyes fixed on Thomas as he ran out of the house, his face twisted with guilt and panic. He had barely asked Webber his first question about the life insurance policy on Emma, and he had already fled the scene.

His instinct kicked in, and Paul took off after him, his heart raced with adrenaline. He sprinted across the yard, his footsteps pounding the pavement as he chased after Thomas's fleeing car.

Paul felt a surge of anger and frustration as he watched Thomas speed away, leaving him to give chase. How could he do this? How could he abandon his daughter and his wife in their time of need?

As Paul drove, his tires screeched as he took the winding roads, his mind filled with thoughts and emotions. He was angry, furious that Thomas would run from him like this. Paul was worried, scared that Webber might be involved in Emma's disappearance and that he might hurt her. Paul pushed his car to the limit, the speedometer climbing as he took the turns, his heart pounded in his chest. He couldn't let him get away, not now, not when he was so close to uncovering the truth.

But as he drove, Paul couldn't shake the feeling that he was losing him. The roads were too winding, too narrow, and Thomas knew them too well. He was getting away, and Paul was powerless to stop him.

His mood was dark, his thoughts consumed by anger and frustration. Paul had never felt so helpless, so out of control. He was a detective, a man who had spent his entire career solving crimes and bringing justice to victims. But now, he was just a man, chasing after a suspect who seemed to be always one step ahead.

As he finally lost Thomas on the winding road, Paul felt a sense of defeat wash over him. He had failed, and he didn't know how to make it right. He pulled over to the side of the road, his car idled, and his mind spun with thoughts and emotions.

Paul took a deep breath, trying to calm himself down, trying to think clearly. He knew he had to get back to the station, to regroup and come up with a new plan. But as he sat there, his heart still raced, his mind still reeled, and he knew that he would never give up. He would find Emma and would bring her home, no matter what it took.

Paul returned to town, the clues blended into a grim mosaic. Thomas sought to profit through deception, his wife and child were merely pieces in a vicious game. But the final curtain had yet to fall, and justice would see it end rightly.

As he drove back to town, his mind still raced with thoughts and emotions. He had lost Thomas, but he knew he had to keep pushing, keep searching for answers. And one of the first places he thought of looking was the county records office. Paul had a hunch that Thomas might be involved in some kind of real estate deal, maybe even using the life insurance policy to fund it. And if that was the case, he needed to find out more about Webber's property holdings.

Paul drove to the town's courthouse, a large, imposing building that dominated the town square. The building was a mix of old and new, with a historic facade that dated back to the 19th century, but with modern additions and renovations. The exterior was made of stone, with tall columns and a grand entrance that led to a sweeping staircase.

Paul walked inside, passed through a security checkpoint, and entered the main lobby. The interior was a mix of old and new, with high ceilings, wooden paneling, and modern lighting fixtures. The air was thick with the scent of old books and papers, and the sound of whispers and keyboard typing filled the air. He made his way to the records office, located on the second floor. The office was a large, open room filled with rows of computers and filing cabinets. The walls were lined with shelves, filled with dusty old books and files.

Behind the counter, he saw a friendly face - Mrs. Johnson, the town clerk. She was a stout woman with a kind smile and a warm demeanor. She had worked in the office for over 20 years, and she knew the records like the back of her hand.

"Hey, Paul," she said, as he approached the counter. "What can I help you with today?"

"I'm looking for property records," he said, pulling out his notebook. "I need to find out what Thomas Webber owns in the area."

Mrs. Johnson nodded, her eyes narrowing as she began to type on her computer. "Let me see what I can find," she said.

Paul waited patiently, watching as she worked her magic. She was a master of records, able to find anything in just a few clicks. And after a few minutes, she looked up, a smile on her face.

"Ah, yes," she said. "Thomas Webber owns a few properties around town. Let me print out the list for you."

She handed Paul several sheets of paper, filled with a list of properties and addresses. He scanned the list, his eyes narrowing as he saw a pattern emerge.

As he continued to look through the list of properties owned by Thomas Webber, he noticed a pattern emerging. Many of the properties were located in rundown areas of town, and several were listed as vacant lots. Paul couldn't help but wonder why Thomas would be interested in these types of properties. He showed the list to Mrs. Johnson, pointing out the pattern. "Do you think this is just a coincidence?"

he asked her.

Mrs. Johnson's eyes narrowed as she studied the list. "I don't think so, Paul," she said. "It looks like Thomas Webber has been buying up a lot of properties in the same area. And most of them are vacant lots."

He nodded as he considered the possibilities. "I think I need to investigate these properties further," he said. "Can you tell me more about the area where they are located?"

Mrs. Johnson nodded. "That area of town has been declining for years," she said. "It used to be a thriving neighborhood, but now it's mostly abandoned buildings and vacant lots. There's been rumors of a developer trying to buy up the area, but nothing's ever come of it."

Paul nodded. He had a feeling that Thomas Webber was involved in something shady, and he was determined to find out what it was.

"Thanks, Mrs. Johnson," I said. "You've been a big help. I think I'll go take a look at these properties and see what I can find."

Mrs. Johnson nodded. "Be careful, Paul. That area of town can be dangerous."

Paul nodded goodbye, his mind filled with possibilities. He had a feeling that this list of properties was key to unlocking the mystery of Emma's disappearance. And he was determined to find out more.

He thanked Mrs. Johnson for her assistance and took the

printouts with him. Paul scanned the property records as he was walking down the street until he saw a café. He went into the café for a coffee and continued looking through the list of properties.

As he entered the café, The Seashell Serenity, he recognized the woman behind the counter, Namita Dsilva, the owner of the café, and Webber's mistress!

He quickly devised a plan as he pondered confronting the mistress, and possible accomplice. He thought to himself the name of the café perfectly summed up the peaceful and serene atmosphere that enveloped visitors as they enjoyed the beauty of the island and the delights of the cafe.

 Steamy scents of spice and simmer wafted from within. The moment you step inside, you're greeted by the rich aroma of freshly brewed coffee. The cafe appeared to be a cozy sanctuary, with weathered wooden tables and chairs that bore the marks of countless conversations and shared moments. The walls were adorned with local artwork, which captured the vibrant colors of the island's flora and fauna. Soft, rhythmic music played in the background, creating a soothing backdrop to the gentle lapping of waves against the shore just outside. Namita herself, a warm and welcoming host, moved gracefully between tables, her easy smile put visitors at ease.

The menu offered a tantalizing array of freshly baked pastries, aromatic coffees, and tropical fruit smoothies that reflected the bountiful flavors of the island. It was a place where time seemed to slow down, allowing patrons to savor each moment as they watched the sun dip below the horizon, painting the sky in hues of orange and pink. Namita's cafe was not just a place to grab a bite, it was an experience that captured the essence of island life in all its beauty and tranquility.

At the counter, a lovely Indian woman smiled. "Welcome. How may I help you?"

"Namita?" She nodded shyly. Paul introduced himself. "We need to discuss Thomas Webber. In private, please."

Her smile froze. Eyes darted. She led him to a quiet nook.

"Thomas? I don't understand, we're just friends."

Paul leaned in meaningfully. "I saw you together, Namita. He's married, and a person of interest in his daughter Emma's disappearance."

Her façade cracked. "That monster used me! I had no idea he had a wife. I knew he had a daughter. You must believe me. Since Emma went missing, he phoned me earlier demanding my silence."

So, Thomas sought to contain loose threads. But this game had rules, and justice would be served. Each piece of evidence brought Paul closer to the undeniable truth... "Did Thomas mention any 'ransom,' Namita?" Paul asked pointedly.

She shifted uncomfortably. "Of course not. I told you I don't know anything about…"

"Your eyes give you away," Paul interrupted. "When I mentioned ransom, they flickered with recognition. The truth now, if you please."

Namita took a shaking breath. Her facade fully cracked as tears welled up. "He promised we'd be together once he got the money. He said with Emma gone and Amelia next, we could start over far from here."

Paul leaned forward intently. "So, you knew about his family, and there was a plan. Where is Emma now, Namita? You must tell me so I can help her."

Broken, Namita met his eyes. "After Thomas got the first payment, he took her somewhere secret. Said it was for her safety until the rest arrived. But I think..." Her voice dropped to a shuddering whisper. "I think he means to kill her."

At last, threads were tied into knots. Paul had his first solid lead, and a tiny life hung in the balance. He vowed this game would end today, with Webber unmasked before the eyes of justice.

Fury twisted Namita's grief-stricken face. "He promised me the world, but it was all lies!" she shouted. Slowing her breathing, she met Paul's steadying gaze. "There are other secrets about Thomas you should know."

Intrigued, Paul leaned in. "Go on."

Namita fidgeted as if wrestling with doomed loyalty. Then the dam broke. "His shipping business is just a front," she hissed. "He brings contraband through the port and pays officials to turn blind eyes. Anyone who threatened exposure went missing."

Paul's blood ran cold. Had Emma stumbled upon her father's crimes by accident? "Names, Namita. Give me proof and we'll ensure he can never hurt you again."

Hope kindled in her eyes even as shame had reddened her cheeks. "His partner is Aldous Grant, a powerful politician. They have..." Namita paused. When she spoke again, her voice trembled with the echoes of other lives destroyed in this tangled web of corruption and greed. Seeing Namita would share nothing further, Paul left.

A cunning and dangerous man lay beneath Thomas Webber's façade. But Paul now held the key to unlocking his secrets and bringing the monster to light. Justice would be done, though the depths of its work ran far deeper than imagined. Paul's mind raced as pieces fell into a dire mosaic. Thomas conspired to profit from his child's demise, using Emma as ransom.

But pulling strings behind the scenes was no lone man. Aldous Grant ensured Thomas faced no costs for his heinous crimes. This was no impulsive act but a cold, calculated scheme. Insiders tied to law and business aided the plot, shielding Webber with layers of protection. Yet he had now met his match. Paul would play this game to its fullest, outwitting the monsters at each turn as he closed the nets. Namita proved the first to yank dominoes from Thomas's control, more cracks would follow.

Paul knew he would now have to stay in the shadows after Namita's confession. Leaving, Paul paused outside the café, piecing together the complex layers of deception. A brutal operation had played out using an innocent child as a pawn. But justice would have its say.

Reinvigorated by his conversation with Namita, Paul walked to the police station. He sought out Sergeant Dumas to bring him up to date and to plan their countermoves. Together, they would bring Webber, and whoever else was involved, to justice.

Paul walked into the police station, looking for Sgt. Dumas. He found him at his desk, typing away on his computer. Paul cleared his throat to get his attention.

"Hey, Sgt. Dumas," I said. "I need to talk to you about something."

Sgt. Dumas looked up, his eyes narrowing. "Hey Paul, how are you doing? What do you need?"

Paul took a deep breath, as he tried to gather his thoughts. "I met with Namita, the woman I saw with Webber on the beach the other day. And I think you need to hear what she told me."

Sgt. Dumas raised an eyebrow. "What did she say?"

Paul took a deep breath as he recalled the conversation. "Namita confessed that she's been having an affair with Thomas Webber. And she told me that Webber's plan was to use a life insurance policy to fund his real estate deals. What's more, she said Webber is involved with his daughter's kidnapping."

Sgt. Dumas' eyes widened in surprise. "That's a huge confession! But why would she confess to you?"

Paul shrugged. "I think she's scared. She knows that Webber's capable of anything, and she's trying to protect herself."

Sgt. Dumas nodded, his face serious. "I think I need to bring her in for more questioning to see if I can get more information out of her."

Paul nodded in agreement. "I think that's a good idea. But you need to be careful, Sgt. Dumas. Webber's not going to go down without a fight."

Sgt. Dumas nodded, his eyes narrowing. "I'll get my team together and bring them up to date. We'll bring her in and see what we can get out of her."

Paul felt a sense of relief. They were finally making progress in the case. And he was determined to see it through to the end.

Chapter 5
Widening the Net

The next morning, Paul returned to the Webber home, loaded with more questions than answers. He knew he needed more information. He returned to talk to the staff to see if they knew anything about Emma's disappearance. He had a feeling that someone might be hiding something, and he wanted to get to the bottom of it.

As he walked up the driveway, Paul noticed that the house seemed quieter than usual. The windows were closed, and the curtains were drawn, giving the house a sense of secrecy. He rang the doorbell, and after a few moments, the door was answered by Maria, the Webber's housekeeper. She looked tired and drawn, her eyes red from lack of sleep.

"Can I help you, Mr. Phillips?" she asked, her voice barely above a whisper.

"I'm here to ask some more questions, Maria," he said, his tone firm but gentle. "I need to talk to the staff about Emma's disappearance."

Maria nodded, her eyes dropping to the floor. "Of course, Mr. Phillips. We'll do anything to help."

Paul followed her into the house, his eyes scanning the room. The atmosphere was tense, and he could feel the weight of the staff's secrets. Paul knew that he had to be careful, that he had to tread lightly. But he also knew that he had to push them, to get to the truth.

And he was determined to uncover it, no matter what it took.

Paul began his interview with the Webber's housekeeper, Maria. She had worked for the family for over a decade and seemed fond of both Thomas and Amelia. However, her affection for Emma was clearly profound.

Maria, a middle-aged woman, with sun-kissed skin from her days under the Caribbean sun, her eyes held depths of wisdom, but also a hint of guardedness. She wore her dark hair pulled back in a neat bun, and her hands showed the wear of years of hard work. Paul noticed she was stoic but observant. She moved with a grace that belies her years of service. Despite her loyalty to the Webber family, there was a quiet intensity in her gaze that didn't go unnoticed.

Paul trod carefully in assessing Maria. While her loyalty to the Webbers ran deep, there was a part of him that wondered if she knew more than she let on. Time will reveal where her loyalties truly lie. Maria recounted her usual routines and movements around the time of Emma's disappearance. According to Maria, she saw nothing unusual that day.

Next, Paul questioned Webber's landscaper, Juan, the ever-watchful landscaper. He was a weathered man, with deep lines etched into his face from years of working under the Caribbean sun. His hands bore the calluses and scars of a life spent in manual labor, a testament to his hard work. Juan's eyes were sharp beneath a grizzled brow, always taking in more than he let on. He is reserved but not without a certain intensity. He moved with purpose, each step deliberate and measured.

There was a sense of quiet strength about him, like a coiled spring ready to unleash if needed. As for considering him a suspect, Paul was mindful not to underestimate Juan. His proximity to the Webbers and his inherent knowledge of the island would prove invaluable or deceptive. Like a hidden thorn among the flowers, Paul would keep a watchful eye on him until his role in this intricate puzzle became clear.

Juan claimed to be working in the back gardens when Emma was taken. He seemed nervous under Paul's scrutiny but would provide no helpful information. Paul sensed Juan may know more than he let on, and decided a more thorough look into his background would be merited.

Next was Webber's au pair, Lourdes. She was a young woman

with a gentle grace that belied the turmoil lurking beneath the surface. Lourdes' features carried a delicate beauty, framed by cascading dark hair that fell like shadows around her face. Her eyes, doe-like and curious, revealed a vulnerability that contrasts with the secrets she may harbor. Paul noticed Lourdes was soft-spoken and observant. There was an air of innocence about her, yet Paul sensed a resilience that hinted at a strength beneath her fragile exterior.

She moved with a certain hesitance, as if unsure of her place in the unfolding drama that surrounded the Webber family. Lourdes was indeed a puzzle to unravel. Her closeness to the Webber household and the intimate knowledge she possessed would make her a key player in this intricate web of deception. As Paul gathered more clues, he would keep a keen eye on her, for sometimes innocence could be the perfect mask for guilt.

She also professed ignorance, though tears filled her eyes when she discussed sweet Emma. Paul noted her reddened eyes seemed more pained than the usual response to such loss. When he gently prodded why, Lourdes finally revealed Thomas had made unwanted advances toward her in the past. This added information painted Thomas in an even far more deceptive light.

Finally, the butler, Mr. Jenkins. Paul approached him with caution, considering their last interaction. Jenkin's stoic demeanor hinted at a wealth of knowledge hidden beneath his composed exterior. Paul delicately probed for any insights he might have regarding young Emma's disappearance.

As they spoke, Mr. Jenkins revealed that he had often observed Emma playing on the beach under the watchful eye of her nanny. His keen observations and sharp memory provided valuable details about Emma's routines and acquaintances. While he didn't disclose any groundbreaking information during their initial conversation, he mentioned a peculiar figure that had been lurking near the estate. This caught Paul's attention.

This detail piqued Paul's interest, which prompted him to delve deeper into potential leads near the Webber home. While Mr. Jenkin's revelations didn't yield an immediate breakthrough, they added another layer to the complex web of the investigation, urging Paul to explore this mysterious figure further. Every snippet of information, no matter how seemingly insignificant, played a crucial role in piecing together the puzzle surrounding Emma's disappearance.

As he walked out of the Webber house, Paul couldn't help but feel a sense of unease. The staff's interviews had left him with more questions than when he arrived. There were inconsistencies in their stories, and he couldn't shake the feeling that they were hiding something.

He got into his car and started the engine, his mind raced with the events of the past few hours. He thought about Maria, the housekeeper, and how she seemed nervous and on edge. He thought about Thomas's affair, and how it seemed to be a recurring theme in the case.

And he thought about Emma, the little girl who was still missing, and how he was no closer to finding her.

As he drove to town, he couldn't help but feel a sense of frustration. He had been working on this case for days and still had nothing concrete. No leads, no suspects, no clear motive. It was like trying to find a needle in a haystack.

But he knew he couldn't give up. He had to keep pushing, keep asking questions, until he found the truth.

Paul arrived in town, the streets bustling with people going about their daily business. He parked his car and got out, his eyes scanned the area. He knew he had to talk to the locals, to see if they had any information about Emma's disappearance.

He walked into one of the local diners, the smell of coffee and grease filling the air. He spotted the owner, a gruff old man named Joe, and made his way over to him.

"Joe, I need to ask you some questions," Paul said, his tone firm but friendly.

Joe looked up at Paul, his eyes squinting. "What's going on, Paul?"

"I'm investigating Emma Webber's disappearance," he said, his eyes locked on his. "Did you see anything unusual on the day she went missing?"

Joe shook his head, his face scrunched up in thought. "No, nothing out of the ordinary. But I did hear something strange a few days before she went missing."

Paul leaned in, his ears perked up. "What was it?"

Joe hesitated, his eyes darted around the diner. "I don't know if it's relevant, but I heard Thomas Webber arguing with someone out front. It was late at night, I had just closed, and I didn't see who it was, but it sounded intense."

Paul nodded, his mind filled with the possibilities. This could be the break he needed, the lead he had been searching for.

"Thanks, Joe," I said, my voice sincere. "You've been a big help."

I left the diner, his mind filled with more thoughts and questions. He had to find out who Thomas was arguing with, and what it had to do with Emma's disappearance.

As Paul widened his search, he encountered a local shopkeeper who reported seeing a stranger lurking along the beachside path that led to the Webber property the day Emma vanished. The witness described a hooded figure glancing around furtively before he retreated into the brush. It was the first sign an outsider may have been involved.

Paul redoubled his efforts, determined to identify and locate this mystery person. Time was of the essence as each new avenue was explored. Paul would not rest until he uncovered the whole truth and brought Emma's abductor to justice. Somewhere, answers existed that could save an innocent child's life, and it was up to Paul to find them before it was too late.

He decided to go back to the Webber home and reinterview Maria. There was something about her that didn't sit well with Paul like she was withholding information.

Sitting in the Webber kitchen as Maria went about her chores, Paul pressured her to talk. "I think you have more to say, you know more than you have told me," Paul pushed.

Maria, with tears beginning to well in her eyes, confided more to Paul as they spoke. She admitted Thomas had a controlling nature, obsessively monitoring both household finances and Amelia's movements. Maria also overheard a vicious argument between the couple just days before Emma's abduction. Thomas angrily accused Amelia of ruining his plans with her constant doubts. Amelia sobbed that she couldn't erase the past, to which Thomas coldly replied some things were better left forgotten. Their raised voices carried through the manor until Thomas stormed out, leaving a distraught Amelia behind.

Maria was worried about her mistress's safety as Thomas's temper seemed to worsen. But none could have predicted the dark turn events would take. Paul made note of these revealing details, seeing the new context in the Webber's fractured relationship. Thomas Webber presented an increasingly unstable and volatile persona beneath his polished veneer. As the layers peeled back, a cruel and manipulative man emerged who stopped at nothing to hide inconvenient truths. Paul was determined to uncover just how far Thomas's evil extended and prayed not too late to save an innocent victim from its reach.

He thanked Maria and left. As he was walking to his car, he spotted one of the Webber's neighbors, an elderly woman named Gertrude. She reported noticing an unrecognized SUV parked along the road near the manor on the day of Emma's abduction.

Gertrude was a woman of advanced age, her silver hair elegantly coiffed and her posture a testament to a lifetime of grace. Her eyes, though aged, still held a sharpness that missed little in the bustling island community. Her hands, weathered by time, spoke of resilience and wisdom earned through decades of living. She exuded a sense of refined calm, her voice carried the weight of experience, yet there was a warmth that invited trust and confidence. She moved with a deliberate slowness that belied the astuteness with which she observed those around her.

Despite her age and seemingly frail appearance, Paul did not underestimate Gertrude. Her position as a close neighbor to the Webbers and her keen insights into the island's happenings made her a valuable ally, or a potential adversary. Paul decided to tread carefully as he assessed her role in this intricate tapestry of secrets and lies until all the threads came together to reveal the truth.

What drew her attention, she explained, were the out-of-town license plates. Though Gertrude couldn't provide a full plate number in her advanced age, she remembered three distinct letters: MNX. It was the first concrete clue potentially linking an outsider to the crime. Paul eagerly made note of the partial plates while he gently questioned Gertrude about other abnormalities she may have observed that afternoon. But she saw nothing more amiss apart from the strange vehicle.

Paul thanked her for her cooperation as he felt the first blossom of hope in what had so far been a barren investigation. This small thread, if diligently pulled, would unravel the whole sinister scheme behind Emma's disappearance. Paul was more determined than ever to trace this SUV and identify its enigmatic driver. He wasted no time investigating Gertrude's valuable clue.

A check of registration records back at the police station uncovered the partial plate belonged to Chad Morris, listed as a partner in one of Thomas's shipping concerns.

Paul decided to pay Mr. Morris a visit. Arriving unannounced at Morris's affluent home, the grandeur of the house was unmistakable. The exterior of the estate exuded sophistication and elegance, with sweeping columns framing the entrance and intricately designed wrought-iron gates that hinted at the luxury within.

As you stepped through the imposing front doors, a grand foyer greeted you with marble floors that gleamed under the soft glow of crystal chandeliers. The walls were adorned with priceless works of art, each painting telling a story of wealth and refinement. Plush carpets in rich hues led the way through corridors lined with antique furniture and elaborate tapestries that spoke of a bygone era.

The state-of-the-art kitchen boasted top-of-the-line appliances, polished to a high sheen, and marble countertops that sparkled in the light. The dining room, with its grand table set for a feast, conveyed an air of decadence, with fine China and silverware that spoke of lavish entertaining.

Moving through the house, you would find luxurious bedrooms with canopy beds draped in silk and velvet, inviting you to sink into their comfort. The opulent bathrooms were adorned with gold fixtures and marble accents, which evoked a sense of indulgence and relaxation.

As you stepped outside, the sprawling grounds stretched as far as the eye could see, with manicured lawns, ornate fountains, and a pool that shimmered in the sunlight. The air was filled with the scent of exotic flowers and the gentle rustle of palm trees, creating an oasis of tranquility amidst the opulence. Chad Morris' home was a masterpiece of luxury and sophistication, a haven of comfort and style that whispered of a life lived at the pinnacle of success and refinement.

Paul knocked on the front door and was immediately met by an arrogant butler. He firmly stated that his business was urgent and that he wouldn't be refused. Reluctantly, the butler left to retrieve Chad Morris. Morris soon appeared, his smooth composure flickered to unease upon seeing the ex-detective. He cut an imposing figure, tall and lean, with a ruggedness that spoke of a life lived on the edge. Chad's eyes, like shards of ice, held a steely determination that hinted at a past filled with shadows. His hands, calloused and strong, bore the marks of someone accustomed to hard labor.

Chad exuded a sense of controlled power. Every movement is deliberate, every word measured. There was an aura of danger that surrounded him, a sense that he had seen more than he let on. Despite his intimidating presence, there was a certain charm in the way he carried himself, a hint of charisma that drew attention. Dressed in dark jeans and a worn leather jacket, Chad's attire reflected his rugged exterior. The faint scent of salt and sea clung to him, a reminder of the island's ever-present influence.

He straddled the line between youth and experience. His face bore the weathering of trials endured, but there was also a hint of youthfulness in the way he carried himself, a man shrouded in contradictions, a puzzle waiting to be solved.

Before Morris could protest, Paul confronted him about his SUV being spotted near the Webber crime scene. Morris blustered innocent claims, though his darting eyes hinted at buried secrets.

As Paul applied pressure, Morris's story crumbled. He finally admitted meeting Thomas that day, though refused to say why or what was discussed. But Paul heard the haunted tone that lay beneath Morris's word; whatever transpired clearly troubled the man. Promising discretion, Paul urged Morris to unburden himself for Emma's sake. Morris remained evasive under Paul's questioning, furiously denying any role in Emma's kidnapping. However, his jittery mannerisms and failure to fully account for his movements that fateful day contradicted his claims of innocence.

While Morris insisted he and Webber merely discussed business, Paul's intuition told a different story. Years of experience had taught him to trust such instincts, especially when paired with a suspect's reluctance to cooperate. Morris clearly knew more than he was letting on regarding the circumstances around Emma's abduction. Recognizing Morris might be protecting an accomplice, or himself, Paul would discreetly arrange for his whereabouts and activities to be monitored going forward. If Morris were truly blameless, then surveillance would confirm it. But if he was involved with or sought to aid Webber in any way, Paul would be there to intercept them.

No stone would go unturned in Paul's quest for truth. He departed from this interaction more certain than ever that Morris held crucial answers, whether willingly or not. And Paul was fully prepared to use any means necessary to extract what was needed to save an innocent young girl's life. The interviews had certainly shed light on possible motives and misdirections. But as Paul expanded his investigation, the tangled web only grew more convoluted. Each new questioning unearthed further connections between those involved, whether they intended it or not.

By now, the entire island had mobilized to aid in the search for Emma. Their communal efforts lifted Paul's spirits, though he knew time was short before hope would fade. More than ever, he felt the weight of others' faith in his ability to secure justice.

While at the shoreline, impressed with the turnout of many locals, Paul decided to pay a visit to Thames' shipping office. In speaking with a clerk there, Paul uncovered suspicious financial transactions and a pattern of threats made against those inquiring too closely into company dealings. The clerk revealed overhearing Thomas arrange an afternoon rendezvous that aligned with Morris's unaccounted movements.

Every revelation compounded Paul's belief in a complicated plot with many scheming players. But amid the layer upon layer of intrigue, were answers that could still save a little girl's life. And that was what drove Paul's tireless, growing campaign to expose the whole wicked scheme before it was too late for Emma. As his investigation broadened, Paul saw the true scope of the conspiracy unfolding. This was no simple domestic crime, but a complex web implicating Thomas's business partners and casting shadows on many residents' reputations. It became clear powerful players had worked for some time to exploit this island community and cover up their criminal dealings. Though their schemes had not before touched Paul directly, they had long undermined the safety and well-being of those under his protection.

Now an innocent child's fate hinged on confronting these elusive manipulators on their own turf. But Paul was more determined than ever to dismantle their schemes, using his honed skills and years of dealing with cunning criminals to outwit them at their game.

The Missing Piece: A Paul Phillips Mystery

He had Sgt. Dumas redouble the surveillance on Morris while at the same time, expanding surveillance of Webber's known associates. Each piece fits into a darkening portrait, bringing Paul and these ruthless operatives onto a dangerous collision course. The stakes had never been higher; prevail, and justice would be served along with peace being restored. Fail, and the life of a little girl may pay the price of his misstep.

As night fell on the island, Paul reviewed his findings, exhausted yet driven. Piece by piece, a sinister plan had begun to emerge, one that went far beyond a simple kidnapping or family quarrel. Powerful figures had infiltrated the community through deception and force. But their pretense of control would not withstand the light he aimed to shine on all their misdeeds. Though fatigued, Paul knew sleep would not come easily with a young girl's life still hanging in the balance.

He hardened his focus on the long road ahead, aware that outmaneuvering such cunning criminals would require perfect coordination and planning. Come sunrise, the hunt would intensify with renewed purpose. Paul was more resolved than ever to end the threat of violence haunting this paradise and return its people to the peace they deserved. With determination as his guide, justice, and safety would prevail where darkness had reigned for too long.

Chapter 6

Trail Goes Cold

As several days passed with no new leads, Paul grew increasingly frustrated with the stalled investigation. The kidnappers remained silent, refusing to make contact despite the hefty ransom demands. The demands were exorbitant, totaling a staggering sum of $1 million for Emma's safe return. The demands were conveyed through a series of cryptic messages, initially sent via anonymous emails that directed the Webber family to drop the ransom in a specified location on the island.

Each message carried a tone of threat and urgency, emphasizing the dire consequences if the demands were not met promptly. The demands were further reinforced by disturbing photos of Emma in captivity, heightening the sense of dread and urgency for her safe rescue. The sinister nature of the demands cast a shadow of fear over the investigation, pushing Paul to navigate the treacherous waters of negotiation and deceit in the race against time to bring Emma home unharmed.

Without further evidence or demands to analyze, all previous leads had gone cold. Media appeals and a sizable reward seemed to generate no useful responses from the public either. Whoever took Emma had vanished without a trace, cocooning her in their hidden location. Paul redoubled his surveillance of suspects like Chad Morris, to no avail. Each dead-end deepened the sense of impending crisis. Though Paul and Sgt. Marcel Dumas worked tirelessly, and no further clues emerged. Emma's parents appeared regularly at the police station with tearful pleas, only to leave deflated when nothing new had materialized. The island-wide searches also turned up nothing. Hope had begun to fade with each unanswered question, public anxiety reached a fever pitch.

Paul knew the stakes were rising with each passing hour. Whoever held Emma was growing increasingly desperate and dangerous with so much attention. He intensified his scrutiny of the case files, probing every detail for some overlooked revelation. But for now, the trail had gone cold. Paul feared this silence from Emma's captors more than any demand, and what it might drive them to do next in their escalating panic.

Late into another sleepless night, straining his eyes in hopes of finding an overlooked detail, Paul sat at his desk, surrounded by stacks of files and papers. He was re-examining the case files, trying to find something, anything, that might lead him to Emma. He was in his small office, a comfortable room with a view of the ocean. The sun had set, leaving only a bright moon glow over the island. Paul had spent hours poring over the files, trying to find a new angle, a new lead.

He started with the initial reports, the ones filed by the police officers who first responded to the scene. He read through the statements of the witnesses, the ones who had seen Emma playing on the beach. He studied the crime scene photos, as he looked for any clues that might have been missed.

Next, he reviewed what little forensic reports there were, the ones that detailed the evidence that had been collected from the scene. Paul studied the DNA analysis, the fingerprints, and the footprints. He was looking for anything that might match a suspect, anything that might lead him to Emma.

He also reviewed the interviews he had with Thomas and Amelia, looking for any inconsistencies in their stories. He studied their body language, their tone of voice, and their words. He was looking for any signs of deception, any signs of guilt. As he reviewed the files, Paul started to notice something. A small detail, one that he had missed before. It was an inconsistency in Thomas's story, a small lie that he had told. He couldn't believe he had missed it before.

Even though Paul knew it may not be anything, he still felt a surge of excitement, a sense of hope. He had found something, something that might lead him to Emma. He leaned forward, his eyes fixed on the file, his mind filled with possibilities. He knew he had to investigate further, to follow up on this new lead. He felt a sense of determination, a sense of purpose. He was going to find Emma, no matter what it took.

Continuing with the files in front of him, the gaps in witness statements remained, as ambiguous witnesses selectively recalled information. Physical evidence like fingerprints and surveillance footage also yielded little, leaving Paul with more questions than answers.

Who really saw what during the critical window of Emma's kidnapping? And what were they still hiding? Even the evidence collected from the ransom drop site and Emma's abandoned toys failed to implicate any suspect. Without sufficient proof, Paul couldn't justify aggressive interrogations to crack witness accounts. The circumstantial clues pointing to Chad Morris hadn't panned out either. Days of watching the man yield a boring existence devoted to business led nowhere. All technical surveillance also turned up empty, leaving Morris untouched.

Paul rubbed his tired eyes in frustration. Without that one missing piece to tie accounts together, the trail had grown cold. Every loophole and inconclusive angle only deepened the tormenting silence surrounding Emma's fate. If a break didn't come soon, Paul feared it would be too late for the young girl whose memory drove his determination.

He woke up early the next morning, after another restless night, feeling a sense of determination and purpose. He had an idea and knew he had to act fast. He grabbed his coffee and headed out to his car, the sun just starting to rise over the ocean.

The drive to the newspaper office was a short one, maybe 10 minutes. He took the coastal road; the wind blew through his hair as he drove. The sun shone brightly as it cast a golden glow over the island. As he approached the newspaper office, Paul could see the building in the distance. It was a small, one-story building with a flat roof and a simple facade. The sign above the door read "Island Times" in bold black letters.

He pulled into the parking lot and got out of his car. The exterior of the building was unassuming, but as he walked inside, Paul was greeted by the bustling energy of a newsroom. The interior of the building was a hive of activity, with reporters and editors typing away on their computers. The walls were lined with newspaper clippings and photos, and the air was thick with the smell of coffee and paper.

The Island Times not only reported news about the happenings on St. Anne but a few of its neighboring Islands as well. Paul walked up to the reception desk and introduced himself to the receptionist, a friendly woman with a warm smile.

"Hi, I'm Paul Phillips, and I'm here to see the editor about a missing person's case."

The receptionist nodded and picked up the phone. "Let me just call the editor, and he'll be right out."

A few minutes later, a tall, thin man with a kind face walked out of his office. "Hi, Paul, I'm John, the editor of the Island Times. What can I do for you?"

Paul pulled out the photo of Emma and handed it to him. "This is Emma Webber, a 5-year-old girl who went missing from the beach a few days ago. I'm working on the case, and I was hoping to get some help from the paper."

John's eyes scanned the photo, and then he looked up at Paul. "Yes, I'm familiar with the case. We ran a few stories about Emma. What do you need from us?"

"I was hoping to get a front-page story in the paper, something that will help spread the word and get people looking for Emma. I have a few details about the case that I think might be helpful."

John nodded, his eyes locked on Paul's. "Absolutely, we'll do everything we can to help. What's the story?"

Paul took a deep breath and began to tell him everything, from the moment Emma was taken to the latest leads he had uncovered. John listened intently, his eyes never leaving Paul's.

When Paul finished, John nodded. "We'll get a story in the paper today, and we'll make sure to get it on the front page. We'll also post it on our website and social media channels."

Paul felt a sense of gratitude towards John and the Island Times. He knew that with their help, he might be able to find Emma and bring her home safe and sound.

A sizeable reward was offered to incentivize any information, no matter how small or seemingly insignificant.

For several days, the story dominated newspaper headlines and TV news cycles across St. Anne and the neighboring islands. Paul hoped it would shake something meaningful loose from witnesses holding back details.

Instead, the deluge of panicked tips and hoaxes only added to the noise. None stood up to verification or offered truly new knowledge of Emma's fate or her captors' identities. Paul spent long hours sifting through each call and report, finding them all ultimately fruitless.

As the initial public frenzy died down, Paul was left more despondent than before. The reward and appeals generated no answers to end Emma's unknown suffering and return to her safe home. With each passing hour, the silence from her kidnappers grew more ominous in what it might soon force them to do in their desperation. Thomas appeared in a widely broadcast television interview, pleading tearfully for his daughter's safe return. He begged the kidnappers directly to show mercy and let the innocent little girl come home.

Watching from his home, Paul studied Thomas Webber's moves with a detective's eyes. Something about the man's delivery seemed practiced, too rehearsed for a distraught father. His eyes also appeared dry, as if he hadn't truly grieved Emma's absence. Could Webber still be deceiving everyone to cover his darker role in these affairs? Paul recalled how the man had slipped away from the previous questioning without expressing real anguish.

Now, as he delivered threats of seeking vengeance also felt hollow coming from Webber. Paul considered the insurance policies still giving Webber motive and wondered if he staged this whole ordeal. Could Thomas Webber really want his daughter Emma eliminated to seal his fortune? Was he still trying to manipulate the investigation away from his culpability somehow? These doubts only deepened Paul's determination to expose the full truth, no matter how powerful or close the perpetrators seemed. Justice would not be thwarted for Emma or the peace of this community.

As the case dragged on without resolution, rumors and distrust began to spread like cancer through the island community.

Whispers of suspect's guilt or innocence took on lives of their own. Fingers pointed accusingly at residents old and new, real, or imagined. Paranoia set in that a depraved individual still lurked among them, holding a child's life in their ruthless hands. Old grievances and envies seemed fresh kindling for wild theories of who truly wanted Emma gone. Security consciousness took on an unsettled edge, as neighbors started seeing threats where once they saw only familiar faces. Paul knew he had to unravel the case quickly to restore calm before mass hysteria took hold. One wrongful accusation fed by rumor could ignite unrest that festered into lasting damage. And in their panicked state, an innocent life might pay the price.

Each day saw the island community become dark reflections of the torment that gripped Paul inside. He redoubled his efforts to find the one path through the web of lies before the truth was lost to chaos forever. For all their sakes, answers had to come and come soon.

As dusk fell yet again with the case remaining cold, Paul felt the weight of failure as it pressed down with each passing darkness. Emma's life now hung by the slimmest of threads, threads frayed by the ineptitude of those meant to protect her.

Alone in his makeshift office at the police station, as streetlights flickered on outside, Paul stared pensively at the evidence wall choking with clues. Somewhere within that tangled mass lay the single fact that could steer him true. But which bit of minutiae held the power to save a little girl from a fate worse than any nightmare?

Paul re-examined surveillance photos and financial records underneath the stark white glow of a single bulb. Willing to perceive some connection missed before, however obscure. There had to be a pattern, no matter how ingeniously disguised, that would lead to Emma's vanishing point and salvation. He knew the responsibility fell heaviest upon him now. With so many having come up short, Emma's frail hold on life depended entirely upon his skills of deduction. Failure was not an option Paul could tolerate as nightfall signaled the slipping of more helpless hours. Sleep would have to wait. Committing himself to solving what others could not, Paul dove back into the puzzle determined to find the missing link. Emma's fate balanced precariously upon the blade-sharp edge of that one elusive breakthrough.

Chapter 7
Doubtful Disclosures

Thomas Webber arrived at the police station with a grim expression. "They've contacted us again," he said gravely, holding up a plastic evidence bag. Inside was a crumpled piece of paper. Paul took the bag carefully and pulled out the letter under the fluorescent lights. The typed words were short and to the point: "You want your daughter back? Bring $500,000 to the old fishing shack at midnight. Come alone." Reading it sent a chill down Paul's spine. He studied the paper closely, noting the common font and lack of identifiable fingerprints.

"When did you receive this?"

"It was tucked under our front door an hour ago," Thomas replied.

Paul examined the envelope but found no postmark or visible DNA evidence. "And you came straight here?"

"Of course," said Thomas. But his eyes darted away, and Paul sensed deception in his response.

Paul's analysis found inconsistencies with the previous notes. "The font is different this time. And demanding another large sum seems reckless."

Sergeant Dumas nodded grimly. "They're getting sloppy or desperate. Both are dangerous for Emma."

Paul feared the kidnapper's unstable state of mind. "I think we need to consider other angles. This latest contact doesn't add up."

He wondered if Thomas was being truthful, or if darker forces were at work beneath the island's surface. Either way, time was running out to save Emma from a kidnapper who appeared to be spiraling out of control. Paul questioned Thomas closely about the ransom note. "The details don't quite add up," he said. "What can you tell me about its delivery?"

Thomas shifted uncomfortably. "I already told you all I know. It had been slipped under the front door when I got home."

"Was there any sign of forced entry?" Paul asked.

"Of course not," said Thomas impatiently. "Now if you're quite finished interrogating me, I have a daughter to save."

"Something you're not sharing could put Emma in greater danger," Paul warned. He leaned forward intently. "Now I need you to walk me through your day step-by-step."

An hour later, Paul was certain Thomas Webber was withholding information. His story had holes and seemed rehearsed. But without proof, Paul had reached a dead end. He thanked Thomas briefly and saw him out, his mind raced to decipher the note's cryptic message and Thomas's evasiveness. Paul was missing something, and Emma's life hung in the balance until he found the missing piece to this increasingly complex puzzle.

Paul returned home and set up his makeshift forensic lab. He used a small room tucked away in the back corner of his house, strategically concealed behind a bookcase in his office. The walls were lined with evidence boards, strings connecting photos and notes which mapped out the intricate connections in the case. There was a sturdy wooden table in the center, cluttered with forensic tools like fingerprint kits, magnifying glasses, and evidence bags.

A microscope sat proudly in one corner, ready to reveal secrets hidden to the naked eye. The shelves were brimming with reference books on criminal psychology, forensic science, and cold cases which helped Paul piece together the puzzle that eluded others. It's here, amid the organized chaos, that he delved deep into the heart of the mystery that currently plagued St. Anne.

Paul had considered this lab his sanctuary, where he could dissect the evidence away from prying eyes, where he could remake sense of the senseless. Every inch of this space echoed his commitment to justice and his unyielding pursuit of truth.

As he looked through the microscope, inconsistencies soon

emerged with the ransom note. The paper fibers didn't match the previous notes. And while those used an old model daisy wheel printer, this letter was laser-printed on a more expensive machine. He examined the envelope next. Same inconsistencies, a laminated surface instead of regular paper. And while the others bore no DNA, he found partial prints here. Was the unidentified match placed there to try and frame someone? Most damning of all, he performed spectral analysis of the ink. The unknown chemicals didn't align with the first communications.

Paul sat back and gripped the table. If this wasn't from the kidnapper, its purpose could only be to point suspicion away from the real culprit. And with Emma's life in the balance, every false clue was lethal.

He needed to re-examine every fact anew, without prejudice. The core of this mystery lay not in what was said, but in what remained unspoken. And during so many deceptions, truth was the most elusive goal. But for Emma's sake, it had to be found.

Paul ran a hand through his hair, his frustration mounted. Someone meant for him to chase false trails while the real perpetrators escaped unnoticed. But to what end? Only one conclusion made sense, the latest ransom was fabricated. And that meant whoever contacted them wasn't interested in money but something far darker. He thought back to Thomas's visit. The man's evasiveness took on new significance against this revelation. Could Emma's own father be manipulating the case? One thing was clear, masters of deception were playing them, with Emma's life the bait and switch.

It was now time for bold action. Paul called Marcel with the damning evidence. "We need to bring Thomas in for further questioning. This latest development suggests he, or an accomplice, is trying to divert us intentionally."

Marcel agreed, though cautioned against rash moves. They would lay their trap carefully. Paul wasn't sure what sinister agenda lurked beneath the island's surface, but he was determined to drag it screaming into the light. For Emma, the kidnapper's games were over, now the hunter would become the hunted. Paul knew he had to double the surveillance on Thomas Webber, determined to uncover the true motive behind the fabricated ransom.

Paul left his house, his mind focused on the task at hand. He needed to surveil Thomas Webber, to see if he would lead Paul to Emma or reveal any clues about her disappearance. He drove to the Webber house, his eyes scanning the neighborhood for any signs of activity. He parked his car a few blocks away, in a spot where he could observe the house without being seen.

He got out of the car and walked to a line of trees next to the Webber property, his eyes fixed on the rear windows. He spotted a small shed in the backyard, partially hidden by a row of trees. It was the perfect spot to observe the house without being seen.

The Missing Piece: A Paul Phillips Mystery

Paul made his way to the shed, his footsteps quiet on the grass. He ducked behind the shed, his eyes adjusting to the dim light. He could see the Webber house clearly, the rear windows and doors in plain sight. As he waited with his eyes fixed on the house, his mind continued to race with thoughts and questions. How long would he have to wait? Would Thomas Webber leave the house again?

The hours ticked by as the darkness deepened, as the sun dipped below the horizon. Paul remained still, his eyes fixed on the house, his ears straining for any sound. And then, just as he was starting to lose hope, Paul saw movement. Thomas Webber emerged from the house, his figure dark and shadowy in the night. He looked around, his eyes scanning the area, before making a quick dash for his car.

Paul watched, his heart raced, as Webber drove away into the night. Paul knew he had to follow him, to see where he would lead him. He slipped from behind the shed, his eyes still fixed on the car's taillights and began to follow him.

Webber weaved the rural roads under cover of darkness, and soon he pulled over near an abandoned shed.

A figure emerged from the tree line, Chad Morris, the partner in Thomas's shipping company. The partners' hurried exchange seemed tense before Morris disappeared again into the night. Webber drove to the marina next and parked far from prying eyes. In the glow of a single light, Paul caught the unmistakable profile of Namita Dsilva boarding Webber's boat.

After a brief conversation, Webber was off again, leaving Namita alone on the boat. The pieces were closing in, but the full picture remained just out of focus. One thing was clear, Thomas Webber's lies hid greater depths, and Emma's life hung on exposing them before the conspirators disappeared into the dark with their terrible secret. It was time for a different kind of confrontation, one where the hunter would not be so easy to evade.

Paul followed Thomas at a distance by car. Then, Thomas parked on the side of the road, camouflaging his car behind some trees and thick brush. Paul had no choice but to proceed on foot and to maintain a discreet distance to avoid detection. He parked his trusty Mustang, shimmering in the moonlight, under the shadow of a gnarled mango tree near the edge of the road. From there, he embarked on a silent journey on foot, his footsteps muffled by the soft sand of the coastal path that hugged the cliffs overlooking the ocean. The walk was a meditative one, the rhythmic sound of the waves below accompanied his steady progress. The moon's gentle glow illuminated the path ahead, casting eerie shadows among the rocks and foliage that lined the trail.

While the walk itself was not physically demanding, the tension in the air lent a sense of foreboding to the otherwise tranquil surroundings. Each step brought Paul closer to uncovering the truth behind Thomas Webber's mysterious movements, which heightened his senses, and sharpened his focus on the task at hand. The treacherous cliffs and the ominous silence of the night added an air of suspense to the nocturnal pursuit, driving Paul onward in pursuit of the elusive answers that lay ahead, as he trekked silently through the thick forest. Webber's mysterious rendezvous demanded answers.

Reaching a remote clearing, Paul deployed his night vision goggles.

To his shock, Thomas conversed heatedly with Chad Morris again. Their hostile gesticulations suggested threatened exposure. A glint drew Paul's eye, Morris slipped Webber an envelope crammed with bills. Blood money for Emma's supposed "rescue"? His suspicions were validated, yet one vital piece was missing. Where was the girl? Paul feared their unstable minds threatened her grim fate. He inched closer through saplings, urgency outweighed stealth. Just then, a snap sent birds shrieking skyward. Paul cursed his clumsiness, but it was too late, sharp eyes had seen movement where none should be.

In a breath, Morris drew his revolver and stole into the bushes. Paul fled through treacherous brush as relentless pursuit closed in. A fatal error had blown his covert operation and endangered the mission. Now the conspirators knew they were being watched. With no answers and a young life on the line, Paul faced his gravest failure yet. Unless a miracle spared Emma from their clutches, all hope would die with her in the night. Paul fled through the forest as gunshots cracked the night. He had grossly miscalculated the threat near at hand.

Emma's abduction cut much deeper than a simple ransom

scheme. Greed and vengeance twisted these men into predators seeking her demise. As he burst from his cover, Paul scanned for patrol cars. None came. Where was Marcel? He was alone in facing enemies who now knew their dark designs had been exposed.

Refusing to flee, Paul doubled back under the cloak of darkness. Entering their conversation uninvited had doomed his stealthy tactics, but he would not leave Emma. Paul reached the clearing's edge and peered through the tangled brush. Two silhouettes argued in heated whispers, oblivious to the pair of eyes that had returned. The proof was there to dismantle their elaborate ruse, yet extracting Emma from these madmen alive seemed a miracle. Paul had lost tactical advantage, but not his resolve to defend the defenseless against pure malevolence. Whatever it took, he would draw them into the light and pull this island from the grip of monsters lurking just beneath. For Emma and all their future victims, the game was far from over.

Now it has entered its most deadly stage.

Paul watched in silence as Thomas and Chad continued their argument. Their words were hushed but tensions clearly ran high. Finally, they parted ways into the dark forest, each no doubt deeply wary after the unexpected intrusion.

Alone in the clearing, Paul had replayed all that had transpired, piecing together the dark truths still obscured from view. Somewhere out there, a little girl's life hung by a thread tied to these men's greed and cruelty. He had to make every action count if she was to be saved from their monstrous designs.

Dawn was still hours away, but sleep would not come. Instead, Paul began planning his next move, knowing the margins for error had shrunk to nothing. He would match their cunning and fight fire with fire, stopping at nothing to defend the defenseless. Come what may, justice and mercy would have their day.

Chapter 8

Targeted Search

Paul ducked behind a tree as he continued watching the suspect's home through his binoculars. It had been several hours since dusk fell, and still, there was no sign of activity inside. He was growing impatient for any clue to emerge, anything that would crack this case open.

As he hid behind the trees, watching the suspect's home, Paul couldn't help but think about the long day that had led him to this moment. He had started the day early, with a sense of frustration and desperation. The case had gone nowhere, and he was no closer to finding Emma. He had been over the evidence a thousand times, but just couldn't seem to crack it.

He had spent the morning reviewing the case files, looking for any detail that might have been missed. He had poured over the interviews, the crime scene photos, and the forensic reports. But nothing seemed to stand out. As the day wore on, Paul found himself getting more and more agitated. He felt like he was failing, like he let Emma and her family down.

 He decided to take a break and clear his head. He went for a walk on the beach, as he tried to let the fresh air and the sound of the waves calm his mind. But even the peacefulness of the ocean wouldn't shake off the feeling of desperation. As the day drew to a close, Paul knew he had to do something. He couldn't just sit around and wait for a break in the case. He had to take action.

He decided to conduct surveillance on one of the suspects, a person who had been acting suspiciously in the days leading up to Emma's disappearance. Paul had been watching from afar, but he knew he had to get closer, to see if he could catch them in the act. He spent the late afternoon preparing for the surveillance, gathering his equipment and stakeout gear. He filled his backpack with water, snacks, and a first-aid kit, just in case.

As the sun began to set, Paul made his way to the suspect's house, parking his car a few blocks away and walking the rest of the way. He found a good spot behind some trees, where he could observe the house without being seen.

As he settled in for what would be a long night ahead, Paul couldn't help but feel a sense of determination. He was going to crack this case, no matter what it took. He was going to find Emma, and he was going to bring her home. He took a deep breath and settled in for the long haul. He knew it wouldn't be easy, but he was ready for it. He was ready to do whatever it took to solve this case.

Just when he was considering calling it a night, Paul saw a light that had flickered in the downstairs window. Moments later, the suspect slipped out the back door carrying a shovel and what appeared to be several heavy-duty trash bags. Paul watched curiously as the figure loaded their car and drove off into the night. He ran to his car, jumped in, started it, and tailed the suspect discreetly, wondering where they could be heading at this late hour.

The dark dirt roads offered little illumination as Paul struggled to keep the suspect's taillights in view. Then suddenly they turned onto an overgrown path and disappeared into the thick foliage. Paul slowed and parked a safe distance away before he continued on foot, listening intently for any sounds through the dense forest. Crickets and frogs filled the air, but then he heard something else, distant scraping and dragging. He crept towards the noises silently and finally spotted a clearing up ahead. What he saw made his blood run cold. The suspect was hastily digging a deep hole, as they tossed shovelfuls of soil behind. All the clues had led him here, to a remote spot where the truth was about to be buried along with a little girl's body. After so many nights of failure, justice for Emma was finally within reach. But first, Paul had a possible killer to confront.

Paul approached the figure digging in the clearing, his steps loud enough to be heard but not to startle. When the suspect whipped around, panic and fear filled their eyes at being discovered.

The Missing Piece: A Paul Phillips Mystery

Evelyn Reed, a close friend of the Webber family and a person of interest Paul had grown suspicious of in his investigation. Her name first pricked the edges of Paul's mind like a thorn in the way she hovered near the Webber family, her subtle glances, and too-polished smiles, all seemed too calculated, too rehearsed. As Paul dug deeper into the tangled web of the Webber case, Evelyn's presence lingered like a shadow at the edge of his vision, a whisper of suspicion that refused to be ignored.

Amid the flurry of doubtful disclosures and murky ransom demands, Evelyn Reed's role in the intricate dance of deception became glaringly apparent. Her poised facade cracked slightly under Paul's relentless gaze and questioning, revealing glimpses of a darker truth that begged to be brought into the light. That was the moment when Evelyn Reed shifted from a curious bystander to a key player in the dangerous game of cat and mouse that unfolded before me.

The way she had held herself, the subtle flicker in her eye, it all pointed to someone hiding darker truths beneath a mask of calm. Paul's gut told him there was more to her story, and he was determined to unravel it, inch by inch until the whole of the truth lay bare before him.

Evelyn Reed cut a striking figure on the island of St. Anne. Her aristocratic poise and polished demeanor made her a magnet for attention, yet there was an air of mystery that surrounded her like a shroud. Tall and elegant, with impeccable style that hinted at hidden depths beneath the facade of sophistication.

Her blonde locks cascaded like a golden waterfall, framing a face that seemed perpetually veiled in half-truths and untold secrets. Her ice-blue eyes held a gaze that was simultaneously captivating and chilling, a window to a soul that guarded its darkest corners fiercely. Evelyn's every movement was calculated, every word measured, a facade of impeccable grace that barely concealed the turmoil roiling beneath the surface. She exuded an aura of enigmatic allure, which drew others in with a magnetic pull that belied the danger that lurked in the shadows of her charm.

A woman of contradictions, Evelyn Reed was a puzzle waiting to be solved, a mystery that waited to be uncovered.

"It's over," Paul said grimly. "Put down the shovel and step away from the hole. I know you killed Emma Webber and buried her here. It's time to end this charade."

Evelyn froze as she glanced between Paul and the open grave as if she weighed up her chance of escape. But she must have seen the resolve in Paul's stare and realized further defiance would be fruitless. With a shuddered breath, she dropped the shovel which fell to the dirt with a heavy thud.

"I didn't mean for any of this to happen," she said, hands raised in weak surrender. "You have to understand..."

"The only thing I need to understand is why," Paul cut them off sharply. "Why take an innocent child's life? What possible motive could justify such a heinous act?" He kept his voice dangerously low, and eyes trained on her now-sagging shoulders as he awaited the confession that would finally give Emma justice. All the missing pieces had fallen into place, and the truth would now see the light, however awful it might be.

"She's not dead," Evelyn yelled.

"What?," Paul demanded. "What did you say?"

"She's not dead. It's a ruse."

The weight of a false reality bore down upon Paul as he uttered those words: "Emma Webber, not dead?

It was a moment where shadows of doubt clouded his mind, darkness whispered lies of despair. The deception was a cunning ploy orchestrated by the kidnapper, a veiled attempt to mislead, to muddy the truth. The discovery of false evidence, a carefully crafted illusion of tragedy, had momentarily cast a pall over hope, shrouding Emma's survival in doubt.

As Evelyn told Paul the story, not the whole story Paul noted, the pieces of the puzzle fell into place, as the truth clawed its way from the depths of obscurity, Emma's true fate was revealed. Evelyn's actions raised troubling questions about her intentions. Why would she be digging a hole if Emma was not deceased? The sinister implications lingered in the air, casting a dark shadow over the scene before Paul. Was this a macabre prelude to an unthinkable act, a plan to dispose of Emma's remains in secrecy? Or was it a deceitful ruse, carefully crafted to mislead and obscure the truth behind Emma's disappearance?

Conflicted by the unsettling possibilities that lay before him, Paul knew that unraveling Evelyn's motives would be instrumental in untangling the intricate web of deception that shrouded the case. The chilling implications of her actions spurred him to delve further into the dark depths of the mystery, where hidden truths awaited discovery amidst the shadows of deceit and betrayal.

Chapter 9
Confronting the Calm

Paul wasted no time in bringing Evelyn Reed to the police station for questioning. As he led her into the interrogation room, the suspect appeared disturbingly calm given the grave accusations.

Paul approached Sgt. Dumas, who was sitting at his desk, typing away on his computer. "Sgt. Dumas, I need to talk to you about Evelyn," he said, getting straight to the point.

He looked up at Paul, a hint of curiosity in his eyes. "What about her?"

"She knows more than she's letting on," he said, his tone serious. "I want to interview her, alone."

Sgt. Dumas raised an eyebrow. "You want to interview her alone? Why?"

"Because I think she's more likely to open up to me if it's just the two of us," he explained. "She's already nervous around the police, and with you in the room, she'll be even more on edge. I need to build a rapport with her and gain her trust."

Sgt. Dumas looked skeptical. "I don't know, Paul. We can't just let you go in there and interview her alone. What if she's involved in the kidnapping?"

"I've thought about that," he responded, anticipating Dumas' concerns. "I'll make sure to record the interview, and I'll have a team outside the room, just in case. But I promise you, Sgt. Dumas, I'll get more out of her if I'm alone."

Sgt. Dumas hesitated for a moment, then nodded. "Alright, Paul. But like you said, make sure to record the interview, and keep the team outside the room. And don't go too soft on her, okay?"

Paul nodded, feeling a sense of relief. "I won't, Sgt. Dumas. I'll get to the bottom of this, I promise."

With that, Paul headed to the interview room, ready to get the truth out of Evelyn.

Once alone, Paul launched into a fierce line of questioning. "We have evidence placing you at the scene of Emma's crime. Multiple witnesses saw your car in the vicinity that day. So don't bother denying involvement," he stated bluntly.

She merely stared back with an eerily placid expression, remaining silent. "Say something!" Paul shouted, slamming his fist on the table in frustration. Still, the suspect did not react, staring back with an infuriating look of nonchalance. Reining in his anger, Paul continued in a low, threatening tone. "The game is up. I know you know where Emma is, so you better start talking if you want any chance of leniency."

A ghost of a smile appeared on her lips, further fueling Paul's rage. Leaning forward until their faces were inches apart, Paul growled, "let's stop playing games. You're going down for this, but I can make it easier or much, much worse. The choice is yours."

Finally, Evelyn spoke in a composed, almost congenial tone. "I'm afraid there's been a misunderstanding, Mr. Phillips. While I understand your zeal for justice, I had nothing to do with that poor girl's disappearance." Paul's blood ran cold as the suspect leaned closer, her eyes glinted dangerously. "You really shouldn't go around accusing people without proof. It could... come back to bite you."

Paul stared her down, unwilling to back down. "I have more than enough proof to put you away for life," he warned. "But tell me the truth and I may be able to help you." Who else is involved?"

A momentary flash of panic crossed her face before it smoothed back to calm. "I've already told you everything I know, and that's the truth" she replied.

"Don't lie to me!" Paul snapped, slamming a fist down again. "We have you placed at the scene, I know you know where she is. Now stop covering for your partners and give up where she is!"

Evelyn paled slightly but tightened their lips resolutely. "I acted alone in this. You won't get anything more from me," she stated, a faint crack appearing in her composed facade.

Paul sensed the fissure and pressed harder, recounting the evidence in brutal detail in an effort to shame the truth out of the suspect. As he finished, a visible tremor passed through Evelyn's body, though she said nothing. Leaning in so close their noses almost touched, Paul hissed, "I will break you if I have to. No jury will have mercy on someone who harms a child. Talk or suffer the consequences. The choice is yours."

Paul rose from his chair and loomed over the suspect, utilizing his physical size to intimidate. "Don't think you can outsmart me. I know what kind of monster you are," he growled menacingly. A bead of sweat formed on Evelyn's brow which took away from any beauty that remained, but still she said nothing. Paul slammed his hands onto the wall on either side of the suspect's head, crowding into her personal space.

"It's over! You're going to rot in prison for what you did to that little girl," Paul spat his face inches from theirs.

The suspect shrank back instinctively, her mask of calm finally cracking under the assault. "I... I didn't mean for it to happen, I swear!" she stammered, panic and guilt flashing in her eyes.

Paul leaned in even closer, refusing to allow any respite. "What exactly didn't you mean to do, huh? Stop lying and tell me what you did with Emma!" Paul had finally unnerved a confession out of the culprit, but what dark truths would now come to light?

Just as the suspect broke, a horrifying confession slipped from their lips. "That little bitch had to pay for her father's sins," she sneered.

Paul froze, dread pooling in his stomach. "What did you just say?" he hissed through clenched teeth. Realizing her blunder, Evelyn clamped a hand over their mouth, but it was too late. Paul seized her by the shoulders in shaking fists, rage and disgust causing his vision to blur. "What did Thomas Webber do?!'

When Evelyn only grinned in response, Paul threw her back against the wall with a roar. "Do not make me ask again!" he warned with deadly intent. After a long tense moment, the suspect caved under Paul's ferocity. "Thomas had been embezzling from investors and framing rivals," she spat. "I was just supposed to scare Emma, not..."

Paul reared back in horrified comprehension. "So, you threatened to kill an innocent child for her father's crimes?!" The darkness in this case had grown far more sinister than he ever could have imagined. And now an innocent life may have been lost.

Paul saw red upon realizing Emma's fate was sealed by her father's misdeeds. "Where is she?!" he roared, shoving the suspect against the wall with brutal force.

But the suspect only laughed maliciously. "I don't know, honest," she replied with stark finality. Paul slammed his fists on either side of her head, trembling with rage. "Tell me right now or so help me God, I will end you!" he screamed, losing himself to his fury. When the suspect merely grinned in response, the last of Paul's restraint snapped. Grabbing her by the throat, he squeezed with deadly intent. "Where...is...she?!"

Even as Evelyn's face turned purple, the suspect maintained her cruel smirk. "You'll...never find her...in time," she gasped out with their last breath. With an inhuman howl, Paul threw the lifeless body against the two-way mirror, shattering the glass. Panting heavily, he saw his wild-eyed reflection, realization dawned in its place. If Evelyn spoke true, then Emma's fate had been sealed, and her death would be in his hands.

The room seemed to have shrunk around them, the weight of unspoken truths pressed in. The act was a calculated move, a test of determination in the face of deception. During that pivotal moment, no one intervened to halt the course of action. The air hung heavy with unspoken words, with the unrelenting pursuit of justice.

Sergeant Dumas, entrusted with the mantle of authority, was elsewhere, his absence a silent acknowledgment of Paul's methods, a tacit acknowledgment of the necessity of his actions in the pursuit of truth.

The Missing Piece: A Paul Phillips Mystery

The confrontation, while forceful, did not result in severe physical injuries to Evelyn that warranted medical attention. The impact was more on the psychological level, the scars of truth cutting deeper than any physical wound could. The suspect bore the weight of her actions in the form of a shattered facade, the cracks in her armor mirrored the fractures in her carefully constructed lies. It was a battle of wills and words, which left indelible marks that would linger long after the confrontation had ended.

Paul stood frozen, the pieces clicked into a horrifying place. He returned to his temporary office down the hall and pulled up the suspect's file on his laptop with frenzied typing as he searched for any clues to Emma's location. A ding caught his attention, Evelyn Reed had ties to an abandoned mill on the outskirts of town. In a burst of adrenaline, Paul sprinted to his car, peeling out of the lot with a screech of tires. Images of Emma's innocent face spurred him faster towards the unfinished structure looming ahead.

The abandoned mill was a place steeped in shadows and echoes of the past. A dilapidated structure, its once-grand facade now worn and weathered by the relentless passage of time. A looming edifice cloaked in mystery, its broken windows like eyes peering into the souls of those who dare to venture near. The mill, a relic of a bygone industry, stood as a testament to a forgotten era when its gears hummed with purpose and its chimneys billowed with smoke.

Now, it lay silent and forsaken, a ghostly reminder of a forgotten legacy. Located on the outskirts of the island, nestled among overgrown foliage and creeping vines, the mill exuded an aura of desolation and decay. Its halls echoed with the whispers of a thousand untold stories, its rusted machinery frozen in a macabre dance of abandonment.

Slamming the vehicle into park, Paul leaped out with his firearm drawn, his trusty Glock 19, a 9mm pistol that he had carried with him for years. The Glock 19 was a reliable and versatile weapon, perfect for a situation like this. It was compact, lightweight, and easy to handle, making it an ideal choice for a detective like Paul. He had carried the Glock with him for years, and it had become an extension of himself. He knew its weight, its balance, and its capabilities. He had fired it countless times and knew that it would perform flawlessly when he needed it to.

Paul cautiously approached the entrance of the abandoned mill, his senses on high alert, ready to take on whatever lay inside.

The rusted iron door resisted but with a bellowed cry he smashed through, greeted by a dank musty foulness. His heart stopped at a tiny whimper in the shadows. The mill's interior was a labyrinth of crumbling walls and creaking floorboards, a maze of forgotten passages that lead nowhere and everywhere. The scent of damp earth and decayed wood lingered in the air, a melancholic perfume that permeated the very essence of the place.

As Paul stepped into the heart of the forsaken mill, the weight of history bore down upon him, a haunted presence that stirred the echoes of the past. It was here, amid the dust and shadows, that the truth lay hidden, waiting to be uncovered in the cold embrace of neglect.

Through the slit in a wall, Paul spotted a shadowy figure pacing in the next room. He froze, scarcely daring to breathe as the suspect's hulking silhouette passed in front of the grimy pane. There was no mistaking that brooding stance, it was the man who had disturbed Paul so during interrogation. As the figure turned, the dying sunlight fell through a knothole revealing a cruel, familiar face keeping a grim vigil. At that moment, Paul knew with chilling certainty that Emma was inside, at the mercy of this depraved man. All the pieces fell neatly into their wretched place, solving the riddle but condemning its subject.

Paul strengthened his nerves as he crept into the darkened room until he found a vantage with a view of the whole scene. There the shadowy figure paced, while inside his precious prisoner no doubt awaited her grim fate. Paul had to act and act fast before the night enveloped all hope of rescue in black oblivion. Clinging to the wall, Paul watched and waited for his opportunity. As the evening deepened, he knew this may be his only chance to ambush the suspect away from Emma. But then, a rustling from within froze both men in their tracks. Paul held his breath, every muscle taut, as the suspect cocked their head attentively. For an ominous moment, the thickening dusk seemed to constrict around the shack. Then came the faintest whimper, a small, terrified sound that shattered the stillness. Emma.

The suspect whirled as he stared daggers through the wall that separated the child from prey. In a flash he vanished within, reappearing with Emma clutched against his heaving chest. Paul rose slowly to his full height, stepping into view with hands spread wide.

"Let her go," he said steadily. But wild eyes merely narrowed as a cold chuckle rolled out. With deliberate menace, he shifted their burden, and the glint of steel came into view, pressed to Emma's throat.

Marcus Ellis, a figure whose sinister intentions had lurked in the shadows of the investigation. His calculated moves and desperate maneuvers had led him to this climactic moment, a dangerous game of cat and mouse where Emma's life hung in the balance. As Paul closed in on Ellis, the final showdown unfolded, a battle of wills and wits that would determine the fate of the innocent child he held captive.

Running through Paul's mind was the intricate web of deceit and deception that unfolded during the investigation. The connection between Marcus Ellis and Evelyn Reed emerged like a twisted thread binding their fates. As the layers of the case unraveled, it became clear that Marcus Ellis and Evelyn Reed shared a clandestine alliance rooted in shared motives and hidden agendas. Their association traces back to a sordid history of shared interests and intertwined destinies, each playing a pivotal role in the dark tapestry of the crime that had gripped the island.

Ellis, with his cunning schemes and ruthless determination, found a willing accomplice in Evelyn Reed, whose enigmatic charm and calculated poise concealed a heart blackened by secrets and betrayals. Together, they forged a dangerous partnership, their paths converging in a deadly dance of deception and danger. The ties that bound Ellis and Reed ran deep, woven with threads of treachery and deceit that threatened to unravel the very fabric of truth and justice in the relentless pursuit of their own twisted desires.

But there was also the connection that bound the fates of Thomas Webber and Marcus Ellis in a dark and intricate tapestry woven with threads of betrayal and deceit. Ellis, with his shadowy dealings and dubious alliances, had found common ground with Thomas Webber through a shared history of hidden desires and buried secrets. Their connection ran deep, rooted in a world of ulterior motives. Marcus Ellis, with his penchant for manipulation and coercion, saw Thomas Webber as a willing pawn in his dangerous game of deception. Webber, in turn, drawn by the promise of power and influence, became entangled in Marcus's web of lies and deceit, each feeding off the other's vices and vulnerabilities.

Their alliance, shrouded in darkness and stained with blood, proved to be a formidable force in the unfolding drama that gripped the island. As the layers of their connection peeled back, the true extent of their collusion became glaringly apparent, revealing a twisted bond forged in the crucible of greed and betrayal.

But how did all this relate to the kidnapping of Emma? Paul

snapped back to reality as Ellis made a move. "One more move and she's dead," he hissed.

Paul froze, his heart pounded, as the deadly standoff began in earnest. The suspect's brutal laugh snapped the last thread of Paul's restraint. In a flash, Paul launched forward, his gun flying as his shoulder struck Ellis' chest.

Emma screamed as the blade slashed harmlessly behind her. Her kidnapper stumbled backward but caught himself against the wall, a rabid animal at bay. Paul raised his hands beseechingly to the child scrambling away in terror. But vengeance now lurked behind Ellis' maddened eyes, which found his gun just out of reach.

With a roar, he kicked off from the wall straight at Paul, tackling him with the force of a wild beast. His head slammed into the ground, stars erupting behind his eyes. But years of street fighting surged to the forefront, every sense attuned to the knife glinting above.

Paul caught his descending wrist in an iron grip, grunting against the primal force that bore down. But fury lent him strength, inching that murderous point further from his throat by slow degrees. With a bellow, he twisted and felt the blade fly from limp fingers, embedding in the dirt beside him. At that moment, his opponent finally peered into the abyss of their own unmaking. Paul saw madness, then fear, then nothing as his fist met Ellis' face in the final blow. A heavy silence fell as the last echoes of violence faded into the gathering night.

The Missing Piece: A Paul Phillips Mystery

"Emma," he breathed, falling to his knees in front of her.

Scuffed knees drew up to a face that was raw from sobbing. But when those big eyes met him, a faint glimmer of hope kindled within. Paul held out scarred fingers, a small smile peeking through his beard. "It's okay, sweetheart. I'm getting you out of here." Emma threw herself into his embrace with a muffled wail. Paul scooped her up gently as a newborn, trying in vain to brush the knots from her hair. Her tiny body shuddered with relief against his broad chest, safe within the shelter of his arms at last.

As he rose with his precious cargo, Paul carried Emma into the night, leaving that cursed place and its horrors behind forever. At long last, justice and redemption were hers. Paul hurried from that cursed place, Emma's tightened fists bunching his shirt with every shuffling step. But snapping branches and heaving breaths gave chase behind them, growing closer through the gloomy wood.

Paul broke into a loping run, each pounding footfall sending shots of pain through his worn muscles and bones. But there was no time to rest, not with that maddened beast on their trail. He splashed through a shallow stream, praying the cold shock would stall their hunter's momentum. No such luck. Crashing footsteps gained on the bank as he tore through the drenched foliage, every sense strained for the faintest sound of escape.

There, a path, narrow but clear, wound into unknown blackness ahead. Paul drew a steadied breath and plunged into the engulfing dark.

Scrambling roots and gnarled branches whipped at his face and limbs. Only adrenaline bore him onward into that hellish void, feet sure where eyes found nothing. Behind, crashing and snarling signaled their relentlessness.

Paul gritted his teeth and ran faster. At any moment, he expected a meaty hand to grab his shoulder from the choking dark. But somehow, impossibly, they hurtled on into the endless night, the gap between hunter and the hunted slowly widening with each desperate stride.

The forest dissolved into an empty field under a moonless sky. He pushed onward with failing legs, as Emma clung limply to his heaving chest. Behind them, crashes and grunts signaled their pursuer's waning stamina and will to hunt. It had to end, here and now, before the night swallowed them all. Spinning, Paul planted and swung with all his remaining might. Knuckles collided with flesh and bone, sending their assailant sprawling into tall grasses.

This nightmare was over; justice had met madness at last on that lonely field. Emma peered through matted hair, hope dawned as he smiled wearily down. "It's okay. You're safe now." He scooped her up close one final time, and Paul began the long walk from darkness into the warm light of dawn. There, faithful Marcel and his men, and an ambulance, had arrived to bear away the last vestiges of violence and return all souls to peace.

Paul settled Emma's sleeping form into the waiting arms of paramedics and stepped back into the new day. Justice had prevailed through quiet wits and dedication to primal truths. Now, in the wake of evil subdued, healing would begin for all it had left scarred in its dark path. Paul had rescued Emma and subdued the suspect so Marcel could arrest him, bringing justice to the situation.

Chapter 10

Frayed Nerves

The hospital on the island of St. Anne held a rich tapestry of history, woven with threads of resilience and healing that dated back many decades. Originally established as a small clinic to serve the local community, the hospital has grown over the years into a beacon of medical excellence and compassionate care. Its foundations were laid by a group of dedicated physicians and philanthropists who saw the need for a center of healing amid the idyllic beauty of the island. Over the years, the hospital had weathered storms, both literal and metaphorical, emerging stronger and more steadfast in its commitment to serving the needs of the island's residents.

The hospital had witnessed the passage of time and the ebb and flow of life within its walls. From the joyous cries of newborns to the whispered farewells of the departing, it had stood as a silent witness to the highs and lows of human existence. Each corner held a story, each room whispered secrets of hope and despair, of triumph and tragedy.

The Missing Piece: A Paul Phillips Mystery

Despite the challenges that had beset it over the years, the hospital remained a pillar of support and comfort for the community it served. Its history was steeped in the tradition of healing and compassion, a legacy of care and dedication that continued to shine brightly in the faces of those who passed through its doors in search of solace and salvation.

In the stark, antiseptic halls, the scent of disinfectant mingled with the quiet hum of machines and hushed voices. The hospital itself was a beacon of hope and healing, a sanctuary amidst the chaos of the outside world. Its walls, painted in calming pastel hues, bore the weight of countless stories of pain and recovery, a testament to the resilience of the human spirit.

As Paul entered Emma's hospital room, the soft glow of sunlight filtering through sheer curtains bathed the space in a warm, comforting light. The room itself had been a haven of quiet reassurance, while the gentle beeping of monitors provided a steady rhythm to the stillness.

Emma lay on the pristine sheets, her small form a stark contrast to the sterile surroundings. Despite the ordeal she had endured, there was a sense of peace in her expression, a quiet strength that belied her tender years. Her condition, while fragile, held the promise of healing and renewal, a testament to the resilience of the human spirit in the face of darkness.

The room itself was sparsely furnished yet imbued with a sense of serenity. A vase of fresh flowers adorned the bedside table, their vibrant colors a stark contrast to the clinical white of the room. The gentle hum of the air conditioning provided a soothing backdrop to the quiet vigil that unfolded within those walls, a beacon of hope amid a time of uncertainty.

The heart monitor beeped steadily as Emma slept, pale but peaceful in the hospital bed. Paul watched over her, lost in thought. His cellphone rang, which jarred him from reflection.

"Phillips, it's Marcel. Any news?"

Paul updated him on Emma's condition. Marcel relayed to Paul, "The suspect resisted arrest but is in custody now. I'll question him once the medics clear him." Marcel sighed heavily. "This island has seen too much darkness over the past few weeks.

"Paul, you need to go home and get some rest," Dumas said, his voice firm but concerned. "You've been at the hospital for hours, and we've got everything under control."

"I'm not leaving until I know Emma is safe," he said, his voice unyielding.

"We've got officers outside her room, and we're keeping a close eye on her," Dumas reassured me. "She's in good hands."

"That's not enough," Paul said, his voice firm. "I want to make sure she has police protection, 24/7 until she's out of the hospital."

Dumas sighed, and Paul sensed his frustration. "Paul, we can't provide that level of protection without a specific threat. You know how it works."

"I don't care how it works," Paul replied, as his voice rose. "I want to make sure Emma is safe, and I won't leave until that's guaranteed."

There was a pause, and Paul could sense Dumas weighing his options. Finally, he spoke.

"Fine, Paul. I'll arrange for a police officer to be stationed outside her room, 24/7 until she's discharged. But you need to promise me you'll go home and get some rest. You're not doing anyone any good by running on fumes."

Paul nodded, even though he knew Dumas couldn't see him. "I'll go home, but I'm holding you to that promise. Emma's safety is my top priority."

"I understand, Paul," Dumas said. "I'll make sure it's taken care of. Get some rest, and we'll regroup in the morning."

Paul nodded again as he disconnected the call, his mind raced with thoughts and questions. But he knew he had to trust Dumas, and he had to trust that Emma would be safe.

"Mr. Paul?"

He turned to see Emma's eyes fluttering open, her small voice weak but determined. Paul rushed to her side, his heart racing with excitement.

"Emma, sweetie, you're awake!" he exclaimed, his voice soft and gentle.

Emma's eyes locked onto Paul's, her gaze filled with confusion and fear. "W-where am I?" she stammered.

"You're in the hospital, Emma," he explained, his voice calm and soothing. "You've been through a lot, but you're safe now. You're safe."

Emma's eyes welled up with tears, and Paul could see the fear and uncertainty etched on her face. "I don't remember," she whispered, her voice trembling.

"It's okay, Emma," Paul reassured her. "You don't have to remember everything right now. Just rest and focus on getting better. We'll figure everything out later."

Paul jumped as the door to Emma's room burst open. Much to his relief, it was Amelia. His eyes were fixed on Amelia as she ran into the room. Her face was etched with worry and fear, her eyes red-rimmed from tears. She had been waiting for this moment for what felt like an eternity, and Paul could sense her anxiety and desperation.

As she entered the room, her eyes scanned the space, taking in the beeping machines and the sterile hospital air. And then, her gaze fell on Emma, lying in the bed, her small body fragile and still.

Amelia's face crumpled, and she let out a sob, her body shook with emotion. She rushed to Emma's side, her arms outstretched, her eyes fixed on her daughter's face.

"Emma," she whispered, her voice trembling. "My baby, my baby."

Emma's eyes fluttered open, and she looked up at her mother, her gaze filled with confusion and fear. Amelia's face contorted in a mixture of sadness and relief, and she reached out to stroke Emma's hair.

Paul stood back, as he watched Amelia and Emma as they shared a moment of tender reunion. The air was thick with emotion, and he felt the weight of their love and devotion.

Amelia's tears fell onto Emma's face, and she kissed her daughter's forehead, her lips trembling with joy. Emma's eyes began to droop, her eyelids growing heavy, and Amelia's gaze never wavered, her eyes fixed on her daughter's face. In that moment, Paul knew that Amelia's world had been turned upside down and that she would never be the same again. The pain and fear of the past few days had taken a toll on her, but in that moment, she became reunited with her daughter, and that was all that mattered.

As he watched, Paul felt a sense of relief that washed over him, and he knew that this was just the beginning of a long and difficult journey. But for now, at that moment, all that mattered was that Emma was safe and that she was back with her mother, where she belonged.

Emma's gaze drifted to the side of the bed, where her mother was sitting, holding her hand. "M-mommy?" she whispered.

As Paul watched, Emma's eyes began to droop, her eyelids growing heavy.

"I'm tired," she whispered, her voice barely audible.

"I know, sweetie," Amelia said, her voice soft. "Just rest. You're safe now."

Emma's eyes closed, and she drifted off to sleep, her small hand still clutched in her mother's. Paul stood back, watching as Amelia stroked her daughter's hair, her face filled with a mix of sadness and relief.

He knew that this was just the beginning of a long and difficult journey, but at that moment, he felt a sense of hope and determination. He was going to find out who did this to Emma, and he was going to make sure they paid for their crimes.

As Paul left the hospital, he decided not to go home, but instead, he drove to the police station where Ellis was being interrogated.

He walked into the police station, knowing he couldn't go home, not yet, not until he had some answers. Paul spotted Dumas at his desk, typing away on his computer, and walked over to him.

"Dumas, I need to talk to you," he said with a firm voice.

Dumas looked up, his eyes narrowing slightly. "Why are you here and not home?"

"I want to be in on the interrogation of Ellis," Paul said, his voice direct.

Dumas raised an eyebrow. "You're not a detective anymore, Paul. You're a civilian."

"I know that," he said, his voice calm. "But I've been working on this case, and I have a feel for it. I think I can get something out of Ellis that your team might not."

Dumas sighed, his expression skeptical. "Paul, we've got trained professionals who can handle this. You're not objective, you're too close to the case."

"I'm exactly what Ellis needs to see," he countered. "A retired detective who's been working on the case. I can push his buttons and make him think I know more than I do. And I can get in his face, make him squirm."

Dumas raised an eyebrow, clearly considering Paul's words. "Okay, fine," he said finally. "But you have to promise me one thing: you have to follow protocol, and you have to let us take the lead. This is our investigation, not yours."

Paul nodded as his heart raced with anticipation. "I promise. I just want to help get to the truth."

Dumas nodded a small smile on his face. "Alright, let's do this.

But don't think you're running the show, Paul. You're just a guest star."

He smiled, a sense of determination washing over him. "I wouldn't have it any other way."

Paul entered the interrogation room where the disheveled Ellis glared back, defiant. "Let's talk," Paul began calmly, taking a seat. "Why'd you do it?" Silence. Paul leaned forward, hardening his gaze. "I rescued Emma while you cowered alone in the jungle. Answer for your sins."

A sneer. His nonchalance ignited Paul's ire. "Nothing else will undo your pathetic life now," he shot back. "Why don't you stop wasting my time?" The man faltered, rage and fear warred on his face as Paul pinned him with his stare. Finally, he spoke a wretched confession pouring out with damning detail. Paul listened stoically, absorbing every word as the full tragedy unraveled before him at last.

The man spat contemptuously. "Thomas Webber hired me to scare them, not hurt the girl! But then she wouldn't stop crying…"

Paul stiffened. "Hired you for what?"

"He was having an affair and wanted a divorce. But the wife threatened to take him to the cleaners. Said if anything happened to the kid, he'd get the life insurance and the business."

The pieces fell into horrifying alignment. "Go on."

"Thomas said scare them really bad, make it look like an outsider did it. Paid me half up front and the rest if I took the girl far away for a few days." His voice dropped. "Only...she just wouldn't stop screaming..."

A chill crept up Paul's spine. Thomas's evils ran deeper than imagined, corrupting others with mercenary sin. The island's true demons were closer than anyone knew, leaching poison into families and lives without care or conscience. His mission was clarified before the last mystery fell into place at last.

The man hung his head in final confession. "Said his partner helped plan it all."

Paul leaned forward. "What partner?"

"Aldous Grant. Runs the fishing ports and owns half the island. He's a politician. A crooked politician. Thomas was skimming money for years, selling under the table. The only way out was to disappear with the cash."

A knock on the interrogation door sounded. Paul turned to see Marcel's grim face, framed in the doorway. Aldous Grant was gone, fled in the night, it seemed, leaving destruction in his wake once more.

But not for long. Paul vowed to hunt these demons to the ends of the earth. The final confrontation was coming.

"Paul, I have alerted all units," Dumas said grimly. "We are moving now, with force. I have men on their way to Webber's house to bring him in. Want to come along?"

"Try and keep me away!"

Within minutes squads of officers descended on the Webber estate, bursting through doors and gates. Paul and Marcel stormed the great room, weapons drawn, to find Thomas poised at the bar.

"Thomas Webber, you're under arrest for conspiracy, kidnapping, and whatever else I can make stick," Dumas announced coldly. "Come quietly."

Thomas sneered. "Do you have any proof, sergeant? It'll be your word against mine."

Paul pulled Ellis' signed confession from his pocket, slapping it on the bar. "Checkmate. Hands behind your back, now!"

Fury twisted Thomas's face as cuffs locked into place. He struggled violently. "You ruined everything! I'll see you dead for this, I swear!" Paul and Marcel wrenched him roughly from the house as they shoved him toward a squad car.

"Tell it to the judge, Thomas. Your reckoning is at hand at last. Justice will be served for Emma, and all the other innocent souls you harmed along your way." The long night was finally ending.

At the station, Marcel and Paul watched through the one-way glass. Thomas paced like a caged animal until Sergeant Leclair, St. Anne's lead police interrogator, entered. "The jig is up, Thomas. Confess and maybe they go easy."

"I don't know what you want!" Thomas growled.

Leclair slapped down the evidence. "Your partner sang. It's over."

Thomas's deflated, haunted eyes found his reflection in the glass. His fiendish deeds warped even his own image.

Sgt. Leclair was a seasoned detective on the island of St. Anne, known for his sharp investigative skills and no-nonsense approach to solving cases. With a reputation for thoroughness and dedication to upholding the law, Sgt. Leclair was a respected figure within the police force, often called upon to handle complex and high-profile investigations. His steely gaze and unwavering commitment to justice made him a formidable presence in the field, earning him the trust and admiration of his colleagues. Despite his gruff exterior, he possessed a keen intellect and a deep sense of duty, driving him to pursue the truth at all costs.

In the tumultuous world of crime and intrigue that engulfed the island, Sgt. Leclair stood as a beacon of order and discipline, a stalwart defender of law and order in the face of chaos and uncertainty. His presence commanded respect and instilled confidence in those around him, making him a pillar of strength in the fight against crime and injustice.

Paul barely breathed as the dam broke and Thomas's fevered confession poured out, each sordid detail twisting the knife further in the community's heart. "I never meant to hurt Emma...but Amelia found out about us, and said she'd take everything. I just wanted it to end!" Thomas dissolved into wretched sobs. He admitted to the affair, the only affair his wife found out about was with Evelyn Reed, a figure whose enigmatic charm and calculated allure had ensnared him in a web of forbidden desires and hidden betrayals. The tangled affair between Thomas and Evelyn was a dark secret that lay at the heart of the mystery surrounding the Webber family, their entangled destinies weaving a tapestry of deceit and deception that threatened to unravel the very fabric of their lives.

Paul exchanged a loaded look with Marcel. Justice had its due at long last. The healing could now begin in earnest for this island and all its scarred inhabitants. The long night's shadow lifted for good. Paul watched Thomas's breakdown, through the one-way glass, as he felt empty.

In the hallway, Paul looked at Marcel, who was smiling, "It's done," his friend said quietly.

Paul sighed. "The truth is out. But its cost…"

"Paul, I don't know how to thank you," Marcel said, his voice sincere. "You've done what we couldn't. You've brought justice to this island, and now we can finally rest easy."

Paul felt a surge of sadness and satisfaction. He looked away, trying to process my feelings. "It's not about me, Marcel," he said in a low voice. "It's about Emma, and her family, and all the people who were affected by this crime. It's about justice, not about me."

Marcel nodded, his expression understanding. "I know that, Paul. But you have to admit, you played a crucial role in bringing Webber to justice. You have a way of seeing things, of understanding people, that's... unique."

He felt a pang of guilt, of shame, as Paul had thoughts about his past mistakes, his failures. He thought about the cases he had botched; the lives he had ruined. "I've made mistakes, Marcel," his voice barely above a whisper. "I've failed people, failed victims. I don't deserve your praise."

Marcel's expression softened, and he placed a hand on Paul's shoulder. "We all make mistakes, Paul. But it's how we learn from them, how we grow, that matters. You've grown, Paul. You've learned. And you've used that knowledge to make a difference."

He looked up, meeting Marcel's gaze, and for a moment, felt a sense of peace, of redemption. Maybe, just maybe, he had finally found a way to make up for his past mistakes.

In the amber dusk, Paul walked to the hospital to visit Emma. When he walked into her room, he found her coloring books spread out as she drew contentedly.

"Paul!" She beamed. He hugged her gently. "You're doing so well. Almost time to check out, huh?"

Emma smiled briefly, and then it faded. "Back home...without daddy."

Paul's heart clenched. "You won't be alone. "And I promise, Emma, there will always be someone to keep you safe, Mommy, Maria. And you can call me anytime, for anything."

Emma Webber, the heart of the mystery that gripped the island of St. Anne, a young girl of tender years whose innocence and resilience shone like a beacon in the darkness. At the age of five, Emma possessed a delicate yet determined spirit that belied her fragile appearance. With golden locks that cascaded like sunlight and eyes that sparkled with a curious light, Emma's beauty was a reflection of the purity and grace that resided within her. Her cherubic features held a hint of mischief and wonder, an infectious joy that warmed the hearts of those around her.

Emma's personality blended seamlessly to form a unique and endearing character. Despite the traumas she had endured, her spirit remained unbroken, her courage never wavered in the face of adversity. She possessed a gentle kindness that touched all who crossed her path, a generosity of spirit that knew no bounds. In Emma, there was a zest for life, a boundless energy that radiated from her like a beacon of hope. Her laughter, like a melody that danced on the wind, carried the promise of brighter days ahead. Emma's resilience and strength of character made her a symbol of hope and renewal in a world shrouded in shadows, a reminder that even in the darkest of times, light could still prevail.

Her small hands squeezed his hands tightly. "Family helps the family. That's what Maria says."

Warmth spread through Paul at the truth in her words. "She's right. Now rest, I'll be back to see you off tomorrow."

Emma snuggled into bed with a contented sigh, tracing horses on her cast. Paul watched from the doorway, feeling her steel core beneath scars only love could heal. This island was indeed his home, its defense, his sacred duty forevermore.

Chapter 11

Closer than Known

The trial was scheduled to begin, and Aldous Grant was still on the run. Paul had to find him to finally put an end to this nightmare. Aldous thought he could slip away into the shadows unnoticed, but Paul had other plans. It all started with a small detail from a witness, a confidential informant Paul had known for several years who mentioned seeing someone resembling Grant at a local hotel, behaving rather suspiciously.

The Blue Coral Inn, an appealing establishment tucked away on the outskirts of town, was a place seeped in the salty air of the island and kissed by the gentle tropical breeze. The inn stood as a weather-worn haven with its wooden facade painted in shades of azure to mimic the shimmering sea. Within, the lobby boasted sand-colored tiles cool against one's feet, while seashell trinkets adorned the reception desk, whispering tales of the ocean's mysteries.

The rooms, each named after a different marine creature, held a charm of their own with pastel-hued walls and rustic wooden furniture.

The windows framed picturesque views of swaying palms and the distant lull of the waves which lured guests into the tranquility of island life. At night, the inn transformed, with soft lantern light that cast shadows that danced on the walls like silhouettes of elusive sea creatures, adding a touch of mystique to the serene atmosphere. The Blue Coral Inn was not just a place to rest one's head but a sanctuary where the whispers of the ocean lulled weary souls into a peaceful slumber beneath the starlit sky.

Paul coordinated the raid on the Blue Coral Inn with Sgt. Dumas and with the cooperation of the Inn's management. The air was filled with concern when they cornered Aldous Grant; it was a moment etched in suspense and tension. The air hummed with anticipation as Dumas and his team, armed with precision and determination, positioned themselves strategically around the Inn. As Paul and his team prepared to breach through the doors, the sound of waves crashed outside which seemed to echo the adrenaline that coursed through the team's veins. With practiced coordination, they stormed the Inn, each step calculated and synchronized to ensure there was no room for error. Bursting through the door of Aldous' room, he put up fierce resistance, his desperation palpable in the air as he sought to evade capture.

However, against the backdrop of chaos, Paul and his team's training and resolve prevailed. There was a brief scuffle, a flurry of movement, and shouts as the team closed in on him with unwavering resolve. In the end, Aldous Grant, faced with the unwavering force of justice, surrendered peacefully. The tension dissipated as he realized the inevitable, and with a sense of bitter acceptance, he laid down his arms. No one was seriously hurt in the raid, which was a testament to the expertise and professionalism of the team that had been assembled to bring Aldous Grant to justice.

Paul stood in the hotel room, his eyes fixed on Aldous Grant, who was now in handcuffs, his smug expression finally replaced with a look of shock and fear. Dumas was reading him his rights, his voice firm and official.

"You have the right to remain silent. Anything you say can and will be used against you in a court of law. You have the right to an attorney. If you cannot afford an attorney, one will be appointed to you."

Grant's eyes darted back and forth, his mind raced as he realized the gravity of his situation. "I want a lawyer," he spat, his voice venomous.

Paul smiled, and a sense of satisfaction washed over him. "You're going to need a good one," he said, his voice cold.

Dumas nodded, his expression stern. "We'll take him in, Paul. You can go home and get some sleep. We'll handle the rest."

He nodded, his mind still filled with the events of the day. He knew that he had to be in court the next day, to testify against Webber and Grant and ensure that justice was served.

As Paul left the hotel room, he couldn't help but think about the evidence they had gathered, about the web of deceit and lies that Grant had spun. He knew that it would be a tough battle, but he was ready.

The next morning, Paul arrived at the courthouse, his heart pounded in his chest. He took a deep breath as he readied himself for the trial ahead.

The courthouse where the trial was to be held stood as a bastion of justice, its imposing facade a testament to the solemnity and gravity of the proceedings within. Located in the heart of the island's bustling town center, the courthouse commanded attention with its neoclassical architecture and grand Corinthian columns that soared toward the sky. As one entered the courthouse, a sense of reverence enveloped the visitor, the echoes of justice rang in the hallowed halls. The polished marble floors gleamed under the soft light that filtered through stained-glass windows which cast colorful patterns on the walls that whispered tales of trials past.

Within the courtroom, a sense of anticipation hung in the air, the wooden benches lined with expectant faces awaiting the unfolding drama. The judge's bench, elevated and stern, presided over the room like a symbol of authority, its gavel poised to dispense justice with a swift and steady hand. The jury box, a row of somber faces, watched intently as the trial unfolded, their duty clear.

The legal teams, clad in sharp suits and earnest expressions, presented their arguments with conviction and eloquence, each word weighed the gravity of truth. In this crucible of justice, the truth would be revealed, and the fate of those involved would be decided by the impartial hand of the law. The courtroom was a stage where lives hung in the balance, where justice stood as the guiding light in the darkness of uncertainty, a beacon of hope in the face of adversity.

As he walked into the courtroom, Paul saw Grant sitting in the defendant's chair, his eyes fixed on the judge, filled with hatred and contempt. Paul smiled, a cold, calculating smile as he whispered, "It's over, Grant. You're going down."

The judge entered the courtroom, and the trial began.

Paul's eyes were fixed on the judge declaring that Grant had entered into a plea agreement. As he read out the terms of the plea bargain agreement. The room was silent, the air thick with anticipation.

"And so, the defendant, Aldous Grant, pleads guilty to the charges of kidnapping and conspiracy to commit murder," the judge said, his voice firm and serious.

The room erupted into a collective gasp, the sound of shock and disbelief filling the air. Paul couldn't believe what he was hearing. Grant, the mastermind behind the kidnapping and attempted murder of Emma, was pleading guilty? He glanced around the courtroom, taking in the reactions of the others. Amelia's eyes were wide with shock, her face pale. Thomas Webber's eyes were fixed on Grant, his expression a mix of anger and fear.

The judge continued, his voice outlining the terms of the plea bargain. "In exchange for his guilty plea, the defendant will receive a sentence of 20 years to life, with the possibility of parole after 15 years."

The room was silent once more, the weight of the sentence sinking in. 20 years to life was a long time, but it was still a lighter sentence than what Grant deserved. But then the judge dropped the bombshell. "Additionally, the defendant has agreed to testify against Thomas Webber, providing evidence and testimony that will aid in his prosecution."

The room erupted into chaos, the sound of murmurs and gasps filled the air. Paul couldn't believe what he had just heard. Grant, the man who had orchestrated the entire kidnapping and attempted murder, was going to testify against Webber? He glanced over at Webber, who sat in the courtroom next to his lawyers, his eyes fixed on Grant. His face was pale, his expression a mix of shock and fear.

Paul felt a sense of satisfaction wash over him. This was it, the final nail in the coffin. With Grant's testimony, they would finally have the evidence needed to put Webber away for good.

The courtroom erupted into chaos once more, the sound of reporters and lawyers talking and shouting filled the air. Paul watched as Grant was being led out of the courtroom in handcuffs.

Philip DeLizio

The courtroom still buzzed with an anxious energy as the trial Webber commenced. The prosecuting attorney stood as a pillar of determination and resolve, his presence commanded attention and respect. Clad in a sharply tailored suit that spoke of his professionalism and attention to detail, every line and crease of his attire mirrored the precision with which he approached his role in the trial. With a demeanor that was authoritative and composed, the prosecuting attorney exuded an air of confidence that instilled confidence in those around him as he presented his opening arguments. His gaze, sharp and penetrating, seemed to pierce through the veil of deception, as he sought out the truth with unwavering focus.

His voice, a resonant timbre that carried across the courtroom with clarity and conviction, rang with the weight of the law. Every word that fell from his lips was measured and deliberate, each argument crafted with the precision of a master strategist. Behind the facade of professionalism, however, lay a fierce sense of justice that burned like a flame within him. The prosecuting attorney was not merely a legal advocate but a champion of truth, a warrior for the voiceless and the oppressed, a defender of righteousness in a world plagued by deceit. As he stood before the judge and jury, his resolve never yielded, and his determination never wavered. The prosecuting attorney embodied the very essence of justice, a beacon of hope and strength in the pursuit of truth and accountability.

The Missing Piece: A Paul Phillips Mystery

Paul sat near the back as he observed everything closely. The prosecution began by laying out the intricate plot hatched by Thomas Webber, Aldous Grant, and their conspirators to defraud the islanders and cover up their crimes. One by one, witnesses recounted the deceit and violence orchestrated by the defendants. Namita Silva testified about Thomas's scheme to use Emma's ransom to start a new life together. Chad Morris told of accepting bribes to enable the corruption.

Even Lourdes, the Webber's au pair, revealed Thomas's unwanted advances and threats meant to ensure her silence. But the most damning evidence came from the defendants' own words. Recordings from the warehouse revealed Aldous and Thomas casually discussing past wrongdoings as if they were discussing the weather. Handwritten logs detailed monetary payoffs and schemes to destroy enemies.

When it was the defense's turn, even slimy maneuvers couldn't counter the overwhelming proof. Thomas shouted denials but his partners stayed calm, resigned to their fates. The defense attorney cut a striking figure amidst the sea of legal minds and impassioned arguments. Dressed in a tailored suit that spoke of sophistication and refinement, every detail of his attire exuded an air of understated elegance that signaled his expertise and experience in the field of law. His demeanor was one of quiet assurance and calm confidence, a mask of professionalism that concealed a keen intellect and sharp wit. With a gaze that held a hint of mystery and calculation, the defense attorney projected a sense of cunning and strategic acumen that marked him as a formidable adversary in the arena of legal battles.

His voice, a smooth timbre that carried a hint of charm and persuasion, held the power to sway opinions and shape narratives. Each word that fell from his lips was laced with nuance and sophistication, each argument crafted with the precision of a master craftsman. Beyond the facade of composure and poise, however, lay a wellspring of passion and dedication to his craft. The defense attorney was not merely a legal defender but a champion of the underdog, a voice for the marginalized and misunderstood, and a protector of justice in a world rife with uncertainty and ambiguity. As he stood before the jury, his gaze unwavering and his resolve unshakeable, the defense attorney embodied the spirit of advocacy and the pursuit of truth, a force to be reckoned with in the complex dance of legal proceedings and moral dilemmas.

The trial encompassed five intense days in the courtroom, a whirlwind of legal battles and emotional testimonies that culminated in a dramatic conclusion of justice. The proceedings unfolded with a mix of tension, revelation, and resolution, as the truth emerged from the shadows of deception and despair.

During those five pivotal days of the trial, Paul's routine was marked by a relentless pursuit of truth and justice. Each morning, he would arrive at the courthouse before the proceedings began, the weight of the previous day's events still pressed upon his shoulders like a burden he willingly bore. As the courtroom came to life with the buzz of anticipation, he meticulously reviewed his case notes, each detail scrutinized and analyzed with the precision of a seasoned detective. The echoes of past investigations resonated in his mind, urging him forward in his quest for redemption and closure.

Throughout the trial, his days were consumed by a whirlwind of testimonies, cross-examinations, and legal maneuverings. Paul observed the witnesses with a discerning eye, seeking hidden truths in their words and unraveling the tangled web of deceit that threatened to obscure justice. In the heat of the courtroom battles, he remained a steadfast presence, his instincts honed by years of experience guiding him through the twists and turns of the trial.

When it was his turn to testify, he often engaged in fierce debates with opposing counsels, his arguments sharp and incisive, his determination staunch in the face of adversity. During breaks in the proceedings, Paul would steal moments of solitude, seeking peace in the quiet corridors of the courthouse. There, amid the whispers of justice and the echoes of the past, he would reflect on the day's events, strengthening himself for the challenges that lie ahead.

As the sun set on each day of the trial, Paul would leave the courtroom with a sense of weary satisfaction, knowing that he had fought with every fiber of his being for the truth to prevail. The shadows of the courtroom would follow him into the night which would haunt his dreams with visions of justice served and the relentless pursuit of redemption.

Each afternoon, after the intense trial proceedings concluded for the day, Paul found peace in a quaint little bistro tucked away on a cobbled street near the courthouse. The bistro, known as "La Belle Échappée," conveyed an old-world charm with its rustic wooden beams, flickering candlelight, and the soft strains of jazz music that filled the air. He would always take a seat at a corner table by the window and would gaze out at the street, watching the people go about their business as if all was right with the world. The ambiance of the bistro was cozy and inviting, a welcomed respite from the rigors of the courtroom drama.

The menu at "La Belle Échappée" was a culinary delight. They offered a tantalizing array of dishes that ranged from hearty cassoulet to delicate seafood bouillabaisse. On those quiet afternoons, he would often indulge in a comforting bowl of French onion soup, its rich broth and gooey cheese topping warmed his soul with each savory spoonful. To accompany Paul's meal, he would partake in a glass of full-bodied red wine, a vintage that the sommelier at the bistro had recommended with great enthusiasm. The wine's velvety notes danced on his palate, a symphony of flavors that complemented the flavors of the meal perfectly.

As he savored each bite and sip, the stresses of the day slowly melted away, replaced by a sense of contentment and peace. The gentle hum of conversation around him, the clinking of glasses, and the soft laughter of patrons created a symphony of serenity that enveloped Paul in its warm embrace, a fleeting moment of respite amid chaos.

On the final day of the trial, the prosecution gave his closing statements. He methodically tied each piece together to prove the complex web of graft and greed that had ensnared so many.

The jury was dismissed for their deliberations. Paul figured he had some time to take a walk and stretch his legs. After being gone for only an hour, Paul's cellphone rang. It was the prosecuting attorney, "Paul, the jury's back" was all he said. The swift return of the jury caught Paul off guard. Their quick deliberation struck a chord of surprise within him, hinting at the intensity of their conviction or perhaps the clarity of the evidence presented during the trial. Such rapid decisions in serious cases always evoked a sense of curiosity and anticipation, which left Paul filled with nerves and hope as the fate of the accused hung in the balance.

Paul walked into the courtroom as the jury was being seated. After they received their instructions from the judge, the jury foreman read the verdicts. It was unanimous: guilty on all counts.

Gasps and applause filled the courtroom as karma was served. Paul watched Thomas Webber being dragged away, his charm and power demolished at last. Darkness had finally been vanquished from the island, and a new future could dawn for all. After the trial concluded, Paul left the courthouse with a lightened spirit. However, his work was not yet done. He decided to visit Emma at the hospital.

As the courtroom emptied in the aftermath of justice served, Paul lingered behind taking it all in. He gazed out at the light of the setting sun, symbolic of this dark chapter that had come to a close. As he stepped outside, the warmth of the fading rays embraced him. Around the courthouse, people huddled in animated discussion, joy, and relief visible in their expressions. Others simply embraced, as they reveled in the healing embrace of community. His eyes searched the crowds and scenes of celebration, finding smiles that outshone the sun. Laughter rang out once more, devoid of shadows' chill. Through it all, an essence of hope had emerged, signs that even after madness darkness would not erase the light within.

As he looked around, Paul noticed a familiar figure waiting for him. It was Emma, who stood beside her mother, Amelia. His heart skipped a beat as he realized that Emma was out of the hospital, and she was smiling at him.

"Emma!" he exclaimed, his voice filled with joy. Paul rushed over to her, sweeping her up in a big hug. "You're out of the hospital! I was so worried about you!"

Emma giggled, her eyes shining with happiness. "I'm all better, Paul! The doctor said I can go home now!"

He sat her down and looked at Amelia, who was beaming with pride. "How is she?" he asked, his voice filled with concern.

Amelia smiled. "She's doing great, Paul. The doctors say she's made a full recovery. We're just so grateful to have her back home."

Paul nodded as he felt a sense of joy and happiness wash over him. "I'm so glad to hear that, Amelia. You must be relieved."

Amelia nodded, her eyes filled with tears. "We're just so grateful to you, Paul. You saved Emma's life. We'll never be able to thank you enough."

He shook his head as humility washed over him. "It was nothing, Amelia. I just did what anyone would have done in my situation."

Emma tugged on his hand, her eyes shone with excitement. "Paul, can we go get ice cream now? I've been thinking about it for weeks!"

Paul laughed, "Of course, Emma. Let's go get ice cream!"

As they walked away from the courthouse, he felt a sense of satisfaction and happiness. Justice had been served, and Emma was safe and sound. It was a good day.

Through it all, Emma's spirit stayed as bright as the Caribbean skies. Though darkness had come, it could not extinguish her flame or this community's. They had weathered the storm together and emerged stronger on the other side. As Paul watched the mother and daughter bond, he knew their island would continue its recovery.

They walked into the ice cream store and the bell above the door jingled as they entered. The store was a colorful and lively place, with bright pink and blue walls adorned with pictures of ice cream cones and sundaes. The air was thick with the sweet scent of waffle cones and melting ice cream.

Emma's eyes widened as she scanned the menu, her face lit up with excitement. "Wow, they have so many flavors!" she exclaimed.

Amelia smiled, laughing at her daughter's enthusiasm. "What's it going to be, sweetie? Do you want a cone or a cup?"

Emma thought for a moment, her brow furrowed in concentration. "I want a cone, please! With sprinkles!"

Paul smiled as he ordered a cone for himself as well. "I'll get the ice cream, Amelia. You and Emma can pick out the toppings."

Emma clapped her hands, her eyes shining with excitement. "Yes! I want rainbow sprinkles and a cherry on top!"

Amelia laughed as she helped Emma pick out the toppings. "You're going to make a mess, kiddo," she teased.

Emma giggled, her face lighting up with mischief. "That's the best part!"

As they walked to a table, Emma couldn't wait to dig in. She took a lick of her ice cream cone, her eyes widened in delight. "Mmm, this is so good!"

Paul smiled as he took a lick of his own ice cream. "I know, right? This is the best ice cream in town."

Amelia sat down beside them, taking a sip of her coffee. "You two are certainly enjoying yourselves," she said, laughing.

Emma nodded, her face covered in ice cream. "This is the best day ever! We solved the mystery, and now we're having ice cream!"

Paul chuckled, wiping a bit of ice cream off Emma's nose. "You're a mess, kiddo," I teased.

Emma giggled as she took another lick of her ice cream. "I don't care! This is too good!"

As they sat there, enjoying their ice cream and each other's company, Paul felt a sense of contentment wash over me. This was what it was all about - solving the mystery, bringing justice to those who deserved it, and enjoying the sweet treats in life.

Emma asked, "Paul, can I get a bite of your ice cream?"

"Emma, you have your own ice cream! Don't be greedy!"

"But I want to try your flavor too!"

Amelia intervened, "Emma, let Paul enjoy his ice cream in peace. You have your own delicious cone."

"Fine, but can I ask Paul something?"

"What's up, kiddo?"

"Paul, can we have a sleepover at your house soon? I promise I'll be good and not make a mess!"

"Emma, that sounds like a lot of fun. But you have to ask your mom first, okay?"

"Mom, can I? Pleeease?"

"We'll see, sweetie. Maybe soon."

"Yay! I'll be good, I promise!"

"I'm sure you will, kiddo. Now let's focus on enjoying our ice cream," Paul responded.

One last task remained before Paul's island duties ended. He returned to the police station that had become his home base after the ice cream store.

There on the wall, evidence photos, and documents chronicled the long path to truth. Paul gazed upon familiar faces, some guilty, others who'd bravely shared pieces forming the whole. Threads of betrayal, collusion, and greed are woven into a tapestry of deceit. Each clue fit seamlessly, pointing to only one culprit, Thomas Webber, and his depraved partners. Satisfied their schemes were fully revealed, Paul began dismantling the case files. As scraps fell into the bin, so did any doubts. Justice had been swift and thorough. The innocent was left whole while ill-intentioned men paid their due.

Thanks to community courage and perseverance, light had banished darkness from these shores. As Paul switched off the lights in his makeshift office at the police station, serenity finally settled upon his heart. His mission had been fulfilled, the people safe, and the evil ones defeated. Now a hero could retire, assured that on this island, good would always triumph over wrong. The dawn of a bright future had emerged at last.

As he was leaving the station, Paul bumped into Sergeant Dumas. "We couldn't have done it without you," Dumas said, shaking Paul's hand earnestly.

Paul nodded in acknowledgment of the team's effort. "Dark days brought this community together, bringing justice to the forefront."

"Especially for young Emma. That resilience gives me hope for the future." Dumas smiled, his eyes crinkling. "Our island is healing Paul. Know you'll always have a place here as long as you live here."

Warmed by the thought, Paul bade his friend farewell. Outside, the night breathed calm over the familiar streets. As he walked, snippets of conversation drifted from homes lit with cheer. Families rebuilding, sharing laughs and dreams of brighter tomorrows.

This place was no longer just where he lived. In defending its people, this tropical Eden had become part of Paul's soul. Wherever the road led, the light and love of St. Anne would stay in his heart forever. For now, his work here was done. The future, like the seas beyond the shore, lay beautifully unknown.

As Paul strolled the beach, his favorite spot, he gazed out at the gentle waves. The evening wind carried memories of battles won, and bonds forged in strife. This land would forever be his home, but the work of healing had only begun. Evil may not haunt the streets anymore, yet its scars still lingered. He would ensure no soul would ever face the dark alone, especially children like Emma. His commitment extended beyond any particular case. The people's safety and happiness were his charge. If threats emerged again, he would stand strong with Dumas at the front lines.

For now, there was comfort as he watched the sun's final rays give way to star-dusted skies. A new day would dawn which would unveil possibilities of smiles Paul had not seen in many years. His job here may be fulfilled, but his purpose had just begun, to see these people he now counted as family, walk in a light that would never fade.

And so, the hero's watch continued, guarding the shores of his paradise. As the moon rose over the tranquil waters, Paul felt relief and sorrow in his heart. While justice had been served, its effects would echo long after. Innocents like Emma would bear scars from the harsh lessons that no child deserved. Yet from suffering sprang humanity's greatest strengths - compassion and resilience to lift each other from even the darkest nights. This community had such spirit in abundance, but guiding hands were still needed.

Chapter 12

Aftermath

Weeks had passed since the trial, and Paul visited Emma and Amelia regularly to see their progress. He was pleased to find that Emma was smiling more often now. Though the memories of that terrible time still haunted her dreams at times, she had coped remarkably well with Amelia's love and support. Paul sensed that a strength within the young girl had helped her withstand such evil and emerge resilient. While scars may remain, her spirit seemed as bright as ever.

Emma delighted in telling Paul about her schoolwork and time with friends. To see her enjoying the carefree days of childhood again filled Paul with relief.

Paul sat on the couch, surrounded by the warmth and comfort of Amelia's living room. Emma sat next to him, her bright eyes shone with excitement as she told him all about her day at school.

"Mr. Paul, I learned about shapes today!" she exclaimed, her voice bubbling with enthusiasm. "We did a big puzzle, and I got all the shapes right!"

Paul smiled as he felt a sense of pride and joy as he listened to her. "That's amazing, Emma! I'm so proud of you. What were the shapes you learned about?"

Emma's face scrunched up in concentration as she thought about her answer. "We did squares, and circles, and triangles... and... and... rectangles!" she exclaimed, her face lighting up with pride.

He chuckled, impressed by her ability to remember all the shapes. "Wow, you're a genius! What was your favorite part of the puzzle?"

Emma's eyes sparkled with excitement. "I liked putting the shapes together! It was like a big game. And my friend Olivia helped me, and we worked together and... and... it was so much fun!"

Paul smiled again, with a sense of warmth and happiness as he listened to her. "That sounds like a great time, Emma. I'm so glad you're enjoying school. What else did you do today?"

Emma's face lit up with a mischievous grin. "We had snack time, and I had goldfish crackers, and they were so yummy! And then we played outside, and I ran so fast, I felt like I was flying!"

He laughed, filled with joy and wonder as he continued to listen to her. "You're a regular superhero, Emma! I'm so proud of you."

Emma's face beamed with pride, and she leaned over to give Paul a hug. "I love you, Mr. Paul," she said, her voice muffled against her chest.

He hugged her back, as he felt a sense of love and gratitude towards this little girl who had stolen his heart. "I love you too, Emma. You're an amazing kid, and I'm so lucky to be a part of your life."

After Emma finished talking about her day, she jumped up from the couch and ran off to play, leaving Amelia and Paul alone. Amelia smiled as she watched her daughter go, and then turned to Paul.

"Thanks for listening to her, Paul," she said, her voice soft and appreciative. "She loves talking to you about her day."

He smiled as he felt a sense of warmth and connection towards Amelia. "I love listening to her," he said, his voice genuine. "She's such a bright and curious kid. You're doing a great job with her, Amelia."

Amelia's face lit up with a smile, and she leaned over to hug me. "Thanks, Paul. That means a lot coming from you. You've been a huge help to us, especially after everything we've been through."

He hugged her back, with gratitude and respect toward this strong and resilient woman. "I'm just glad I could be there for you, Amelia. You and Emma have been through a lot, and I'm honored to be a part of your lives."

Amelia pulled back, her eyes shone with tears. "We're honored to have you in our lives, Paul. You've been a rock for us, a source of comfort and strength. We don't know what we would have done without you."

The normally hard façade of Paul, if only temporary, fell away as he felt a lump form in his throat as he looked at Amelia, sincerity, and gratitude in her eyes. "You're an amazing mother, Amelia," he said, his voice soft. "You've been through hell and back, and yet you're still standing, still fighting for your daughter's happiness. You're a true hero, and I'm honored to know you."

Amelia's face crumpled, and she burst into tears, her body shaking with sobs. Paul held her, feeling compassion towards her, and let her cry, as he knew that she needed to release all the emotions she had been holding inside.

Though Amelia still struggled with sadness on quiet evenings, she had found relief in being reunited with Emma and friends who had reaffirmed their care and loyalty. The bonds of the community proved as powerful as hoped. With each new day, more smiles replaced shadows on Amelia's kind face.

All across St. Anne, communities organized fairs and fundraisers to raise the spirits and help those still healing. Neighbors spent more time-sharing meals and laughter in each other's homes. The tight-knit bonds that defined the island were reforged through shared sufferings overcome by solidarity. Trust and goodwill had taken root where deceit and fear once haunted. Hope bloomed anew like the island's wildflowers after each rain. Though scars remained on land and souls, the people of St. Anne emerged ever stronger in their unity. Their triumph of light over darkness would stand as an example for all enduring tough times.

Paul said his good-byes, walked to his car, and pulled out of Amelia's driveway, with a sense of relief and closure as he left the warmth and comfort of her home behind. The sun had begun to set as it cast a golden glow over the small island of St. Anne. He drove down the quiet streets and passed by the familiar landmarks of the town: the ice cream parlor, the library, and the town square.

As he drove, he couldn't help but think about the Webber case, and how far they had come. From the initial kidnapping to the final confession, it had been a long and winding road, filled with twists and turns. But in the end, justice had been served, and Emma was safe.

Paul turned onto the main road and passed by the beach where Emma had been kidnapped. He felt a pang of sadness as he thought about the trauma that Emma had endured, but he was also grateful that she was safe and sound.

As he drove into the town center, he arrived at the police station, the small, unassuming building that had been the hub of their investigation. He pulled into the parking lot, as a feeling of nostalgia washed over him. This was where it had all started, where they had worked tirelessly to bring Webber to justice.

He got out of the car, stretched his legs, and took a deep breath of the salty air. He walked into the station and was greeted by the familiar faces of the officers and detectives. They nodded to Paul as he passed, their faces were somber and serious.

He made his way to his makeshift office and to his old desk. A feeling of familiarity came over him as he sat down in the creaky chair. He gathered his files and belongings with a sense of closure as he packed up the last of the Webber case. Paul took one last look around the station with gratitude towards the people and the place that had been such a big part of his life.

And then, he stood up, shouldered his bag, and walked to the front door of the station. Paul bid farewell to the dedicated police team that he had worked so closely with during this ordeal. He was proud to have collaborated with such compassionate public servants, including his friend Dumas.

He was about to leave, his files and belongings gathered, when Sgt. Dumas approached Paul. His face was serious, but his eyes held a hint of gratitude.

"Paul, can I have a minute?" he asked, his voice low.

Paul nodded, setting his bag down on the floor. "Of course, Sgt. Dumas."

Dumas cleared his throat, his expression solemn. "I just wanted to say thank you, Paul. Thank you for everything you've done for us. You've been a game-changer in this case, and I don't know where we would be without you."

Paul felt pride and satisfaction swell within. "It was my pleasure,

Sgt. Dumas. I'm just glad I could help bring justice to the Webber family."

Dumas nodded, his eyes serious. "You did more than that, Paul. You brought hope to this town. You showed us that even in the darkest of times, there's always a way forward. And for that, I'm eternally grateful."

For the second time today, Paul felt a lump form in his throat, this time as he looked at Dumas, and he saw the sincerity and gratitude in his eyes. "You're a good man, Sgt. Dumas," he said, his voice soft. "You've been a great partner throughout this case. I'm honored to have worked with you."

Dumas smiled a small, tight smile. "The honor's been mine, Paul. I'm just glad we could work together to bring this case to a close."

Paul nodded as he felt closure. "Me too, Sgt. Dumas. Me too."

Dumas held out his hand, and Paul took it, shaking it firmly. "Take care, Paul. You've earned it."

Paul smiled with gratitude and respect towards Dumas. "You too, Sgt. Dumas."

And with that, Paul turned and walked out of the police station.

While donning his hat with a twinge of sadness to leave such steadfast comrades, Paul felt only optimism for St. Anne's bright future. He knew the island was in good hands under Dumas' principled leadership. Together with its resilient people, St. Anne would continue healing and thrive. Paul departed the station as he believed he had helped the place he cared for find justice, light, and peace once more.

Once home, Paul walked along the sandy beach as he listened to the soothing lull of waves. As gulls called out, he pondered all that had passed. Though the costs of the corruption that was exposed cut deep, purpose and resilience defined these people. He thought of Emma finding light and Amelia's renewed smile, feeling relief they had prevailed against evil's depths.

Thanks to the many brave souls like Dumas, the island now had banished the killers that poisoned its soul. As he restored safety and belief in fairness, Paul fulfilled his duty as protector. These shores held a beauty soothing to the weariest heart and spirit now. Paul sensed in its sands and palm trees a healing balm for any survivor of life's harshest storms. In helping this place, he called home rediscover joy and goodness, his days found reason once more.

As the moon rose and stars awakened in soft dusk, Paul knew strength and hope would always remain as long as communities supported each other through darkness' hardest nights.

Paul stood on the veranda of his seaside cottage, breathing in the soothing ocean air. So much had changed since he first sought retirement's simple pleasures here several years ago. Through serving these resilient people, they now felt like the family he had searched for. As gulls cried out over the crashing waves, senses were soothed by this place's natural comforts. Lights from the small nearby village twinkled with the warmth of the community. He sensed in their flickers a dawn breaking, bringing fresh hopes for all recovering from hardship's long nights.

Paul's retirement had found a richer purpose. In bringing justice once more to this beloved corner of the earth, his own healing was complete. He knew wherever needs arose, his strength and skills would aid others. As he gazed at the moon that began to rise over the calming seas, Paul's heart was full. This island's beauty and its people had become his own. Though new journeys may come, its spirit would forever stay within his soul.

For now, retirement could truly begin, and with its blessings of love, service, and redemption, life felt richly lived. Paul gazed over the sea, watching as the sunset painted orange and pink hues across the sky. This island had given him purpose once more through its battles against darkness. Though the investigation ended, his commitment to St. Anne and its people would remain.

This remote yet vibrant community had become his own over the challenging months spent unraveling deception and restoring justice. In its natural beauty and resilient spirit, Paul found the home and family he had long sought. While new journeys may come, this place would stay in his heart. Should threats to its safety and goodness ever emerge again, Paul knew he would stand with its people as they had for him, with courage, solidarity, and faith in tomorrow's brighter horizons.

As stars began to wake above, Paul felt only optimism for all who persevered through this most recent storm and embraced each new day's promises. He was confident that through supporting one another, St. Anne would continue healing and thrive. His watch would remain until full peace and light-filled every soul.

A gentle breeze caressed his skin, a breeze that carried the scents of ocean and palm that reinforced his belongings. All was calm once more. With a smile, Paul watched the moonrise, feeling only serenity and gratitude for this blessing of home and community he would always cherish. Paul inhaled the soothing ocean breeze one last time and smiled at the serenity before him. This place breathed new life into his retirement and reinforced his connections to people who now felt like family.

Paul finally reached his home, after his walk had lasted longer than he planned. He sat on his porch, the warm breeze rustled his hair as he gazed out at the sea. The sun had set, and the moon had risen. He held a large rum drink in his hand, the ice clinking against the sides of the glass as he swirled it around.

As he sat there, he couldn't help but think about how much St. Anne had come to mean to him. When he first arrived, he was running from his past, trying to escape the demons that haunted him. But as he settled into the island life, he began to feel a sense of belonging. The people of St. Anne had taken him in and welcomed him with open arms.

He thought about Amelia and Emma, and how they had become like family to him. He thought about Sgt. Dumas and the rest of the police department, and how they had become his colleagues and friends. And he continued to think about the island itself, with its rugged beauty and its laid-back charm.

As he sat there, he realized that he had finally found a sense of home. St. Anne was no longer just a place to escape to; it was a place where he belonged. The people of St. Anne were no longer just strangers; they were his family.

Paul took a sip of his drink, feeling the rum burn down his throat. He closed his eyes, as he let the sound of the waves wash over him. He felt a sense of peace, a sense of contentment, that he had never felt before.

He knew that he would never leave St. Anne. This was where he belonged, surrounded by the people and the place that he loved. He was home, and he knew that he would never be alone again.

He opened his eyes and gazed out at the sea once more. The sun set long ago, the moon had cast a white glow over the waves. Paul smiled with a sense of gratitude and belonging.

This was his home, and he was exactly where he was meant to be.

As the surf crashed and trees rustled, Paul readied for bed. First, a quick check of the locks on the doors and windows. Can't let any unwanted guests disturb his peace. Then, a bit of light reading, preferably something unrelated to crimes. Finally, Paul completed his deep breathing exercises which he used to calm any unwanted thoughts in his mind.

He drifted into a restful slumber. He slept in peace, cradled by the relentless yet soothing pulse of this place now etched into his very being. Dawn would bring new promise, and for him, a future of purpose under the shelter of a beloved sky.

Chapter 13

Old Wounds, New Beginnings

The warm breeze swept across the beach as Paul gazed out at the sunset's gorgeous hues of orange and pink. Six peaceful months had passed since the trauma of little Emma's kidnapping, and the island of St. Anne had fully healed from the scars of darkness. To pass the days, Paul helped the locals repair boats at the dock, shared meals with friends, and volunteered with local causes. He had found serenity in the simple rhythms of each day and delighted in the bonds of community he had formed. Though having retired from active duty some time ago, Paul's instinct to protect remained, he kept a watchful eye and lent an ear to any who needed it.

Amid the unfolding aftermath of the trial, Paul found peace and renewed purpose in immersing himself in the vibrant tapestry of island culture on St. Anne. His typical day began with the soft caress of the early morning sun filtering through the curtains of his quaint island bungalow nestled among the swaying palm trees and the soothing sound of the ocean's lullaby. As the day beckoned with promise, he would embark on a leisurely stroll along the sun-kissed beaches, the powdery sand warm beneath his feet. The salty breeze carried the tang of the sea, mingled with the sweet scent of tropical blooms that dotted the landscape in a riot of colors. Seagulls wheeled overhead, their cries a melodic backdrop to the symphony of nature.

He would venture into the heart of the island's bustling town center, where the vibrant marketplace thrummed with the energy of local vendors and visitors. The colorful array of fruits and spices spilled across makeshift stalls, their rich aromas tantalized his senses and beckoned him to explore further. Among the lively chatter of islanders and the strains of traditional music that filled the air, Paul would sample exotic culinary delights, freshly caught seafood, tangy fruit salads, and fragrant rice dishes that spoke of generations of culinary tradition. Each bite was a revelation, a journey through the flavors and fragrances of a culture as rich and diverse as the island itself.

In the afternoon, Paul would seek refuge in the shade of a palm tree, a well-worn novel in hand as he lost himself in the words and worlds of master storytellers. Could I write a true crime novel? he thought to himself. The rustle of the leaves overhead and the distant murmur of the waves provided the perfect backdrop for his literary escape which transported him to the realms of mystery and intrigue far removed from the troubles of the mainland.

As the sun dipped below the horizon in a blaze of fiery hues, painting the sky in a multitude of colors, he would retreat to a local watering hole, a quaint seaside tavern where the laughter of patrons mingled with the clinking of glasses and the strains of live music. Savoring a chilled glass of island rum, he would raise a toast to the day's adventures and the promise of tomorrow, grateful for the respite and renewal that island life had bestowed upon him.

Most of all, Paul cherished his time with Emma, who had blossomed into a happy child again under Amelia's devoted care. Paul beamed with pride as he watched Emma learn and play without fear. Her smile reminded him of why his efforts were worth it, to shield innocence and allow life to thrive freely once more. The trauma was now a distant memory replaced by sunshine, laughter, and the resilience of the human spirit. Paul knew that wherever life led him next, the soul of St. Anne would stay in his heart as a place of belonging, a place he could always call home.

Now, as the sun had set, Paul heard laughter as it drifted from the beach. He turned from the beach with pangs of hunger reminding him he hadn't eaten in a while, so he made his way to the local diner that he often frequented. The Coral Reef Cafe is a pleasant seaside eatery that exudes a laid-back tropical vibe. Nestled along the water's edge, the diner offered a panoramic view of the azure sea stretching out to the horizon, the gentle lap of waves provided a soothing accompaniment to the dining experience.

As he entered The Coral Reef Cafe, the inviting aroma of freshly brewed coffee and sizzling seafood wafted through the air, mingled with the salty tang of the ocean breeze. The decor was eclectic and whimsical, with colorful seashells and nautical memorabilia adorning the walls all of which created a cozy and welcoming atmosphere.

Ready to take 'his' seat at a weathered wooden table, Paul would normally peruse the extensive menu, which featured a tantalizing selection of island favorites, from grilled fish tacos to coconut shrimp curry. The culinary offerings at The Coral Reef Cafe celebrated the bounty of the sea and the vibrant flavors of the Caribbean, each dish prepared with care and expertise by the talented local chefs.

He would sip on a frosty glass of passionfruit iced tea while he gazed out at the tranquil waters beyond as the sun cast a golden glow over the rippling surface. The gentle hum of conversation and laughter filled the air, creating a sense of community and camaraderie that was as comforting as the delectable cuisine on offer.

In the evenings, The Coral Reef Cafe transformed into a lively hotspot, with live music and dancing under the stars adding a festive touch to the dining experience. The warm glow of lanterns and the twinkle of fairy lights created a magical ambiance, a testament to the island's spirit of joy and celebration that permeated every corner of the diner. The Coral Reef Cafe was not just a place to dine but a sanctuary of island hospitality and culinary delights, a haven where locals and visitors alike could come together to savor the flavors of the sea and the warmth of genuine hospitality that defined the essence of island life.

But this visit to the café would be different. In a good way.

Upon entering, warm greetings filled the air as regulars saw their friend. Paul chatted with the locals, glad to see life returning to normal after last year's trauma. In a corner booth, to his surprise, he found Emma happily chatting with Amelia over milkshakes. The sight of their smiles and laughter warmed his heart. He slid in beside them.

As Paul sat down with Amelia and Emma, the warm glow of the setting sunbathed them in a soft light, casting a serene ambiance over their gathering. The gentle chatter of diners and the distant cry of seagulls created a backdrop of tranquility, a peaceful respite from the shadows of the past that lingered in Paul's mind.

"How are my two favorite ladies doing this evening?"

Emma beamed. "Great! I got an A on my spelling test." Amelia's eyes shone with pride. "We're doing well, Paul. Thanks to you, we can finally heal in peace." Paul smiled gratefully.

For their meal, which Paul insisted on paying for, he opted for a classic island dish, a seafood platter filled with succulent grilled shrimp, buttery lobster tail, and tangy ceviche. The aroma of the freshly caught seafood mingled with the salty sea breeze which tantalized his taste buds with promises of culinary delights. Amelia chose a light and refreshing tropical salad, a medley of crisp greens, ripe mango slices, and toasted coconut, drizzled with a zesty citrus vinaigrette. The vibrant colors of the salad mirrored the joyful spirit that Emma radiated, her laughter filled the air with a melody of innocence and hope. Emma enjoyed a delightful meal of fish and chips, a classic seaside favorite that resonated with the simplicity and joy of childhood innocence. The crispy golden fish fillets and perfectly cooked fries delighted her palate, each bite a reminder of carefree days spent by the ocean, her laughter like music in the air.

Throughout the meal, their conversation flowed easily, a blend of shared memories, hopes for the future, and reflections on the challenges we had faced. They spoke of Emma's resilience in the face of adversity, of the strength that bound them together as they navigated the turbulent waters of life. Along with the clatter of cutlery and the clinking of glasses, a sense of camaraderie bloomed between them, a bond forged in the crucible of their shared experience and the unspoken understanding that connected them at a deeper level. Paul found comfort in the simple pleasures of good food, good company, and the promise of new beginnings that lay on the horizon.

Amelia said it was getting late and they should leave, despite Emma's protests. They bid Paul goodnight and Paul promised Emma he would stop by tomorrow to see her.

After leaving the diner, Paul walked along the shoreline on his way home, memories surfaced of darker times, but sunset had passed, and dawn rose anew for this community. Though shadows lingered, the strengthening bonds of those within gave Paul hope that here, the light would always prevail.

With these thoughts, he sat on the beach as he enjoyed the present moment, surrounded by those who had become family. After a few minutes of quiet contemplation, Paul resumed his walk along the beach, deep in thought. So much had changed since he departed the big city streets years ago, burdened by past failures. Here on the Island of St. Anne, he unearthed redemption through serving this community, protecting the innocent from threats both seen and unseen.

Paul gazed at the sky, smiling softly as he recalled dark days replaced by countless sunrises viewing this very scene. Life's winding journey had led him here, to find peace and comfort among the palm trees and surf, instead of the sirens and concrete of the big city.

The ghosts of his past had been exorcised, leaving him grateful for each day. Though retired from active duty, purpose-filled his days through vigilance and companionship. Old wounds had healed, and in its people, he'd discovered a reason to hope again. As sea winds caressed his skin, Paul knew that wherever the current carried him next, the soul of this place would stay in his heart forever, a reminder that light triumphs over darkness so long as communities stand together. The island's beauty and strength would remain his lullaby through any storm.

With a deep breath of salt air, Paul felt only tranquility. This paradise had become his home, and he, its sentinel, was ready to shield its beauty, until his final sunset. With gratitude in his soul, Paul watched the last rays fade gold upon a thankfully peaceful horizon. He stood, gazed at the night sky, and saw the stars twinkling like a soothing balm. So much had changed these past months. The old wounds that stalked his dreams had eased as purpose emerged serving this place. Forming bonds of care and trust with island folk had salved the pains of failures past. Here, he'd healed through lending aid wherever needed, patching boats, cooking for the elderly, and tutoring eager youths under palm trees.

Simple routines soothed the haunted edges, replacing screams that had echoed down city streets with children's laughter drifting on ocean breezes. This steady anchor offered peace amid life's storms.

And then his cell phone rang.

Paul sat on his porch after his walk along the beach, enjoying the warm breeze and the sound of the waves. He looked down and saw Sgt. Dumas' name is on the caller ID. He smiled and wondered what he wanted to talk about.

"Hey, Sgt. Dumas," he answered.

"Paul, how's it going?" he asked, his voice warm and friendly.

"It's going great, thanks for asking," he replied as he leaned back in his chair.

"I'm glad to hear that," he said. "I wanted to talk to you about something. We've been thinking about creating a new training program for our recruits, and I think you'd be the perfect person to lead it."

Paul was taken aback, surprised by the offer. "Me? Why me?" he asked.

"Well, you've got a wealth of experience, Paul," he said. "You've been a detective for years, and you've got a great track record of solving cases. Plus, you've got a way of connecting with people that's hard to find. We think you'd be a great fit for the job."

Paul was flattered by the offer, but he was also hesitant. He had been thinking about just taking it easy and enjoying his life on the island. But as he thought about the opportunity, he couldn't help but feel a sense of excitement.

"I don't know, Sgt. Dumas," Paul said, hesitating. "I was thinking about my retirement and just taking it easy for a while."

"I know, Paul," he said. "But we need someone like you. You'd be doing a great service for the community and for the police department. And who knows, you might find that you enjoy it more than you think. And it would not be a full-time job. We would hire you on a consultant basis."

He thought about Dumas' words as he weighed the pros and cons in his mind. He thought about the opportunity to make a difference, to help shape the next generation of police officers. And he thought about the excitement of taking on a new challenge.

"Okay, Sgt. Dumas," Paul said finally. "I'll take the job."

He laughed, a warm, relieved sound. "I knew you'd see it our way,

Paul. Welcome to the team."

Paul smiled as he felt excitement and anticipation. He had a new challenge ahead of him, and he was ready to take it on.

"Thanks, Sgt. Dumas," he said. "I won't let you down."

Paul hung up the phone with a renewed sense of pride and purpose. He had a new role, a new challenge, and he was ready to take it on.

The following morning, Paul started thinking about his new position with the police department on the island. Understanding the need to pass on knowledge and experience to the next generation of law enforcement officers, Paul was happy to share his insights and expertise in a formal training capacity. The chance to impart his skills and mentor aspiring officers resonated deeply with his sense of duty and commitment to justice, igniting a renewed sense of purpose and fulfillment in contributing to the safety and security of the community on St. Anne.

He remained vigilant through training the new officers. With Sergeant Dumas lacking resources, Paul's guidance proved vital in cultivating the next generations' skills. Each day, recruits gather beneath palm trees to learn observation techniques, evidence analysis, and maintaining objectivity amid emotional cases.

Paul ensured a thorough understanding of laws regarding safety and justice. Through practical scenarios, rookies honed instincts and teamwork. Paul felt pride as he saw once troubled youth flourish under structure and purpose and is now ready to serve with empathy and care. Bonds strengthened the force, whose united efforts upheld harmony.

Paul smiled when he saw Dumas' relief knowing the island's protection was secure. Though tired, his energy was renewed as he mentored minds eager to shield paradise. With skills newly learned the recruits now stood ready when trouble stirred. Paul gained peace and comfort as he recognized that his watch continued through the new recruits, now equipped to preserve light and justice.

As he arrived home one afternoon, drained of energy, a pattering of footsteps approached Paul's porch. He turned from the setting sun's last rays to see Emma clutching a Tupperware of cookies, beaming. "We baked these for you! As a thank you," she said, pushing silky hair from her eyes.

"Emma, these look amazing," Paul said, taking a bite of one of the cookies. "You're definitely a talented baker."

Paul's heart swelled as he recalled the shadows that once threatened her innocent smiles. "Emma couldn't wait until tomorrow. She just had to bring these to you today," Amelia said, smiling.

Emma beamed with pride, and Amelia smiled, her eyes shining with happiness. "We're glad you like them," she said, sitting down in the chair next to Paul. "So, how's the new job going?"

Paul leaned back in his chair, taking another bite of his cookie. "It's going well, thanks for asking. I'm really enjoying it."

Amelia's eyes sparkled with curiosity. "What's it like, training the new recruits? I can only imagine it's quite a challenge."

He nodded, taking a sip of his coffee. "It definitely has its moments, but overall, I really enjoy it. I like being able to share my experience and knowledge with the new recruits and help them become better officers."

Amelia leaned forward, her eyes intense. "What kind of duties do you have? Are you still working on cases, or is it more of an administrative role?"

He sat his coffee down and thought about how to answer her question. "It's a bit of both, actually. I'm still somewhat involved in a few cases, but I'm also responsible for training the new recruits and helping them develop their skills. It's a bit of a mentorship role, but I also have to make sure that they're following procedure and doing things by the book."

Emma, who had been quietly listening to their conversation, suddenly spoke up. "Do you get to wear a badge, Mr. Paul?" she asked, her eyes shining with excitement.

Paul smiled, chuckling. "I do, Emma. I wear a badge and everything. It's very official."

Emma's face lit up, and she clapped her hands together. "That's so cool, Mr. Paul! I'm glad you're doing something you love."

He smiled again as he felt a sense of warmth and gratitude towards Amelia and Emma. "I am, Emma. I'm really happy with my new job, and I'm glad I get to share it with you both."

Amelia smiled, her eyes shining with happiness. "We're glad to hear it, Paul. You deserve it."

After Amelia and Emma had left, Paul sat and listened as the ocean's song drifted upon breezes. Waves gentle as heartbeats soothed his past pains with each rise and fall. As he gazed at the vanishing sun's glow upon the water, Paul felt only gratitude, for finding peace and tranquility upon the shores of St. Anne.

Chapter 14

Full Circle

The morning sun had risen lazily over the tree line as Paul swam his usual laps in the calm waters offshore. As he emerged from the surf, he shook the droplets from his hair and reached for his towel. As the damp warmth soaked into his skin, Paul breathed in the coconut-scented breeze with gratitude. Six more peaceful months had passed on the island since the darkness had been vanquished.

After reaching his bungalow, he dressed in a loose shirt and light pants, then made his way up the beach path toward the main road. The sounds of roosters crowed, and children's laughter drifted through palm branches that were heavy with ripe fruit. Rounding the bend, the painted houses and open-air shops of the village came into view, bustling as usual with morning routines.

Paul waved to the bakery owner who had been stacking fresh loaves of baked bread in her window display as he strolled over to a dockside cafe. Taking his usual seat under the awning, he ordered coffee and fruit from the young server, slipping her a generous tip with a wink. As the girl blushed and hurried off, Paul watched sailboats fluttering their sails on the horizon, conveying goods and travelers between blue islands.

The peace of the morning was broken by a familiar voice. "Still causing trouble I see, Paul." Sergeant Dumas smiled, settling into the neighboring chair.

"Just keeping these young ones on their toes," Paul chuckled.

They exchanged pleasantries about the village goings-on before Dumas leaned in, his tone becoming serious. "I have a sensitive matter that could use your expertise if you're willing." Intrigued, Paul nodded to him to continue, curious about what mysteries still lingered beneath the island's tranquil veneer.

Dumas, rubbing the back of his neck. "We've received a troubling report I was hoping you could assist with." Paul nodded, gesturing for him to continue. "The manager of the cruise ship docked in the harbor came to see me today. He said several of their passengers have reported items have gone missing from their cabins overnight." Dumas continued, "There have been multiple thefts that have occurred aboard. Valuables seem to vanish without a trace, causing quite a stir among the tourists. We suspect an insider is involved, someone with access to restricted areas. These thefts are tarnishing the reputation of our tranquil island, threatening the tourism that we rely on." Dumas shook his head. "Empty wallets, watches, jewelry, you name it. All from locked rooms with no sign of forced entry."

Paul stroked his chin thoughtfully. "That does seem peculiar. Any theories on how they're doing this without being seen?"

"None so far," Dumas replied grimly. "The manager is worried it could damage their business if it continues. I know you have...experience in these matters. Would you be willing to take a look? Discreetly, of course."

Intrigued, Paul agreed to help, sensing an opportunity to practice his skills once more for the good of the community. Dumas sighed again. "That's not all, I'm afraid. When we investigated the first reports, things were...mishandled." Paul raised an eyebrow questioningly. "The new officer I put on it got in over his head," Dumas admitted. "Didn't secure the scene properly, lost some key evidence. I had words with him, but the damage is done."

Paul nodded slowly, sensing his friend's frustration. "Without a proper investigation from the start, the case will be much harder to solve."

"Exactly," Dumas agreed. "I could use your expertise if you're willing. Start fresh without the mistakes." For a moment Paul was quiet, considering. His days of mystery-solving were behind him, yet curiosity still flickered occasionally. He knew the importance of justice and security for visitors to the island.

"Very well, I'll take a look and see if anything was missed," he said at last. "No guarantees of success, but I'll do what I can."

Dumas smiled, relieved. "Thank you, my friend. Your insight could be just what we need." Curiosity had stirred in Paul once more.

The next morning, Paul arrived at the station and went to work. Dumas showed him what evidence they had collected, too little, in Paul's practiced eye. He donned gloves and began reexamining each item carefully. Sergeant Dumas showed Paul the surveillance footage of a shadowy figure moving furtively near the cabins where the thefts occurred. Additionally, he obtained witness statements detailing suspicious behavior from a certain crew member known for accessing restricted areas. Combine that with a missing keycard that was traced back to the same crew member, and they might just have their culprit. Time to connect the dots and bring justice to this cruise ship mystery.

The crew member in question, according to the evidence presented by Sergeant Dumas, was Carlos Mendez, a member of the ship's janitorial staff. It seemed his routine cleaning duties conveniently put him in proximity to the cabins where the thefts occurred. "Time to pay Mr. Mendez a visit and see if we can uncover the truth behind these mysterious disappearances."

Mendez was of medium build, with dark hair and a perpetual scruffy beard that added a touch of unkempt charm to his appearance. He had a weathered look about him, which suggested he might be in his late forties. Mendez had been with the cruise ship for a solid seven years, overseeing the janitorial duties with a quiet efficiency that rarely drew attention to his activities. As for a criminal record, all signs pointed to a clean slate for Mendez. However, as Paul knew, past behaviors don't always define present actions. It seemed they may have found their prime suspect or merely a red herring in this intricate game of cat and mouse.

As Paul boarded the ship and located Mendez, he maintained a calm yet authoritative demeanor, keenly observing his every move for any hint of deception. His first question was direct, "Carlos, can you explain your whereabouts during the times the thefts occurred in the cabins?"

Mendez, visibly taken aback by Paul's inquiry, fidgeted slightly before he composed himself. He insisted that he had been following his usual cleaning schedule and had not ventured near the cabins during the said times. Unconvinced by his response, Paul pressed further, "Have you noticed anything unusual happening on the ship recently? Any suspicious activities or individuals that caught your attention?" Mendez's eyes darted momentarily, a telltale sign of unease. He hesitated before claiming ignorance of any unusual occurrences. Sensing a crack in his facade, Paul pursued, "Do you have access to master keycards or know of anyone who might have tampered with the cabins?"

At this, Mendez's composure wavered, beads of sweat forming on his brow as he vehemently denied any involvement in the thefts or knowledge of the master keycards' whereabouts. Despite his protestations, Mendez's nervous demeanor and evasive responses only served to deepen Paul's suspicions. It appeared Paul might be getting closer to unraveling the truth behind these elusive thefts on the cruise ship.

Paul returned to the police station to relay his conversation to Sgt. Dumas. "He knows more than he admitted," Paul began. "Mendez is clearly involved, but I don't think he is acting alone."

Paul wanted to review the rest of the evidence collected by Dumas and his men. After an hour of silent work, he discovered what he was hoping for, a partial fingerprint left on a watch stem that had been "bagged and tagged" but not dusted for prints as it should have been. The watch was found on the floor in one of the cabins, apparently dropped unnoticed by the thief. Taking the print to the records room, he soon had a match to a small-time criminal in their database.

Paul returned to Dumas with the news. "The suspect's name is Luka Williams. Petty thief with a record of B&E going back to his youth. I'd bet this is more than coincidence."

Dumas scratched his chin, thinking. "So, we may have professional thieves, not opportunistic passengers. Good catch, my friend."

After running a check on Luka Williams, it was determined Williams was an intriguing new player in the unfolding mystery. It seemed that Williams and Mendez have a curious association that warranted further investigation. Upon delving deeper into their connection, it became apparent that Williams and Mendez shared overlapping shifts on the ship, with Williams frequently seen engaging in hushed conversations with Mendez in secluded corners. Witnesses reported seeing Williams passing small packages to Mendez discreetly, which raised suspicions of clandestine dealings between the two. Additionally, their movements seemed orchestrated, almost as if they were working in tandem to conceal something nefarious.

This newfound association between Williams and Mendez only added layers to the web of intrigue surrounding the cruise ship thefts. Perhaps their alliance held the key to unraveling the mystery that had eluded the police, and the cruise ship authorities thus far. It was time to confront these two and uncover the truth behind their shadowy dealings.

Relieved at the break in the case, Paul felt the old spark of the hunt reignited inside him. "Now we find our Mr. Williams and have a polite conversation. I believe he can point us to his partner, or partners, and lead us to recover the stolen goods."

Dumas grinned. "Then let the hunt begin."

Paul responded, "To catch these suspects pilfering items from the cruise ship, we need to think like them."

He explained they needed to set up surveillance points at vulnerable areas, possibly bait them with a valuable item, and coordinate closely with ship security to create a tight net. "Once we identify their patterns, we can move in swiftly and apprehend them red-handed," Paul rationalized. "It's about outmaneuvering their cunning with our precision. Let's bring these thieves to justice."

That evening, Paul began a discreet stakeout near the docked cruise ship from the shelter of some palm trees. The surveillance operation at the cruise ship involved strategically placed cameras that covered key areas, the dock, storage facilities, and passenger cabin hallways. Paul's position would vary, coordinating from a nearby vantage point to oversee the operation. Observing patterns and waiting for the suspects to make their move would be crucial. He had to anticipate their actions to outsmart them. The hunt was on, he mused, let's make every move count.

The cruise ship, a grand vessel, gleaming white against the azure waters, with multiple decks stacked high, adorned with rows of porthole windows and expansive open decks. A behemoth of the sea, it spans hundreds of feet in length, housing thousands of passengers in luxurious cabins, entertainment venues, restaurants, and recreational facilities. The ship bustles with activity, featuring pools, theaters, and shops, all set against the backdrop of endless ocean vistas. A floating city, complete with its own vibrant pulse.

A few hours past midnight, he spotted two slight figures boarding one of the vessels with rope ladders. Activating a pair of night vision binoculars, and watching the hidden surveillance cameras, Paul watched as Luka and an accomplice worked methodically down the hallways, pausing at each cabin to test for unlocked doors. One was rewarded, Paul observed their silhouettes enter and begin searching through luggage in rapid, practiced motions. After a few minutes, the pair exited again, a stuffed backpack, evidence of their success. They made their way back to shore without seeing Paul concealed in the dark. He trailed discreetly from a distance as they stowed their winnings in an abandoned shack on the edge of town.

The abandoned shack where Paul followed Luka and the unknown other man was a dilapidated structure, weather-worn and barely standing amid the overgrown foliage that obscured its existence. The shack showed an air of neglect, with its wooden planks peeled and sagging, and the roof displayed gaping holes that allowed streaks of light to filter through. Obviously, abandoned years ago. Located on the outskirts of the island, nestled deep within a dense thicket, the shack seemed purposefully hidden from prying eyes, as if it concealed secrets better left undisturbed. Surrounded by gnarled trees and tangled undergrowth, it bore the marks of isolation and desolation.

To reach this clandestine location, after following Luka by car for a few miles, Paul had to park on the side of the road and navigate a winding path on foot, obscured by thick foliage, each step fraught with the silent whispers of the wilderness. The trek was a test of patience and stealth, treading carefully to avoid alerting his targets to his presence. As he finally reached the shack, Paul hunkered down, concealed among the shadows, awaiting the unfolding of a mystery that promised to illuminate the dark recesses of deception.

As Paul cautiously approached the abandoned shack, the scene that unfolded before him was nothing short of a clandestine rendezvous shrouded in secrecy. Through a crack in the weathered wood, he glimpsed Luka standing with an air of anticipation, a mysterious package clasped in his hands. The stolen items from the ship, glinting faintly in the dim light, were unmistakably nestled within the folds of the package. It appeared that Luka was in possession of the very objects that had gone missing from the cabins, which confirmed Paul's suspicions of his involvement in the thefts. His accomplice, who was not Mendez, was a shadowy figure whose identity remained unknown, stood beside him, their hushed conversation hinting at sinister intentions.

As Paul observed from his vantage point, Luka made a furtive gesture, signaling the completion of their transaction. With a nod, the figure departed, blending seamlessly into the surrounding foliage like a ghost in the mist. Luka, however, chose to remain, his gaze lingered on the package with a mix of satisfaction and apprehension. It seemed he was reluctant to leave the shack, perhaps embroiled in a web of deceit that bound him to this desolate rendezvous point. The revelation of Luka's involvement and the recovery of the stolen items cast a harsh light on the shadows that concealed his actions. It was only a matter of time before the truth unraveled completely, exposing the dark underbelly of deception that had taken root on the cruise ship.

The next morning, Paul and Dumas returned with a warrant. Emerging from the shack, they found Luka and an associate named Rolf. They followed the men through the heavily overgrown jungle down to the water. There, the men began loading a small boat with boxes of stolen goods, clearly planning to flee.

"Hands behind your back, gentlemen," Paul greeted them calmly. The game was up. Dumas snapped on the cuffs with a satisfied grin, another case closed.

Based on Paul's information, Dumas assembled a team to raid the thieves' hideout. That evening, they moved in swiftly as Paul kept watch. Apprehended without a fight, perfect. Meanwhile, bursting through the doors of the abandoned shack were Dumas' men. "Well done as always, sergeant," Paul remarked. A search of the premises revealed caches of stolen wares and evidence of other accomplices.

Back at the station, Paul watched the interrogation through the two-way mirror. Under duress, Luka cracked first, proclaiming their ringleader was notorious thief Diego Morales in exchange for leniency. He also confirmed Mendez supplied the gang with access to the cabins using a stolen key card.

As Dumas stepped in to confirm, Rolf nodded bitterly. "Morales, that rat, always gives up the rest of us in the end," Rolf added that

Morales was known to fence stolen goods overseas, but his whereabouts were currently unknown. Paul smiled as he sensed the climax approaching.

"Not for long. I believe I know how to draw Morales out of hiding." Dumas raised an eyebrow expectantly. "A cunning fox requires an appropriately baited trap. Leave the planning to me."

The next day Paul and Dumas review their plans for the arrest of Morales. Paul still relished the chance to outwit a criminal mastermind and restore ultimate justice for the island. The endgame was unfolding nicely. The meticulous planning to apprehend Morales was a pivotal moment in their quest for justice. The plan was intricately crafted by Sergeant Dumas and Paul, leveraging their collective experience and knowledge to ensure a swift and decisive capture. The operation involved a coordinated effort with Dumas leading his team to surround Morales at a secluded warehouse on the edge of the island. With precise timing and strategic positioning, their goal was to encircle Morales and prevent any chance of escape, cornering him in a trap of his own making.

As the arrest unfolded, Dumas and his officers moved in with precision and expertise, swiftly securing Morales before he could react. Their seamless execution and unwavering resolve ensured that Morales had nowhere to run, which made the culmination of their efforts to bring him to justice all the better. While Paul provided guidance and support throughout the operation, it was Dumas and his dedicated team who orchestrated Morales' arrest as they seized the moment with unwavering determination. Their commitment to uphold the law and safeguard the community was evident in their swift and decisive actions, culminating in the apprehension of a dangerous criminal.

Though Paul stood on the sidelines, his presence loomed over the scene as a reminder of their shared mission to seek truth and deliver justice. The arrest of Morales served as a testament to the collaborative efforts of law enforcement, highlighting the power of teamwork and dedication in the face of adversity.

As the sun began its descent over St. Anne, Paul sat watching from the beach, lost in thought. Though he had embraced retirement and found tranquility here, his aid was still called upon from time to time. Helping Dumas apprehend the thieves had been satisfying, which reminded Paul that his skills could offer value when darkness crept in once more.

The weight of the day's events pressed upon Paul as he reflected on the contrasting closures of the cruise ship thefts and the case of missing Emma. The capture of the cruise ship thieves, while satisfying in its resolution, paled in comparison to the emotional gravity of finding Emma safe and sound. Solving the cruise ship thefts was a testament to the investigative prowess and determination to see justice served. The careful unraveling of the mystery, and the apprehension of the perpetrators, was a triumph of skill and perseverance, a reminder that no crime would go unpunished under the watch of Sgt. Dumas.

The Missing Piece: A Paul Phillips Mystery

And Paul.

On the other hand, the case of missing Emma resonated with a deeper importance, as it stirred echoes of past failures and unfulfilled promises. The relentless pursuit of truth, the haunting specter of a child's disappearance, was a journey fraught with personal stakes and profound implications.

As Paul contemplated the dual closures, he couldn't help but feel a bittersweet satisfaction. The cruise ship thieves may have been brought to justice, but Emma's safe return carried a weight of redemption, a flicker of hope in a world shadowed by darkness. The echoes of past failures may still linger, but at this moment, in this closure, there was a glimmer of solace, a reminder that justice, though hard-won, was always worth the fight.

As the first stars emerged above like gentle eyes watching over the island, Paul knew that wherever life led him, this place would always feel like home. The bonds he'd formed with those who had become family, and the care they showed one another, filled his days with purpose beyond any singular case. His successes here gave renewed meaning to his days and ensured he was never alone, even when paradise's shores could no longer hold him.

As he gazed out at the tranquil horizon of St. Anne, contemplating his future in the wake of the day's revelations, the question of whether to stay on the island as his retirement home was now answered. Yes, he will stay on St. Anne for as long as he can. The gentle sway of the palm trees and the soothing murmur of the waves seemed to beckon Paul to linger, to find comfort in the island's serene embrace.

As Paul charted his course forward, he resolved to strike a delicate balance between embracing the tranquility of retirement and heeding the silent summons of unresolved stories waiting to be unraveled. Paul thought aloud, "Perhaps I will immerse myself in the gentle rhythms of island life, cast my fishing line into the azure waters, lose myself in the pages of crime novels that echoed the echoes of my own battles."

Yet, beneath the veneer of retirement's peace, a flicker of restlessness stirred within him, a silent reminder of the unquenchable thirst for justice that defined him. Whether he chose to remain on St. Anne or venture forth into the unknown, one thing remained certain, Paul Phillips would continue to navigate the mysteries of the human heart, seeking truths that eluded the naked eye, determined to bring light to the shadows that lingered on the horizon.

Printed in the USA
CPSIA information can be obtained
at www.ICGtesting.com
LVHW021510181024
794066LV00012B/372